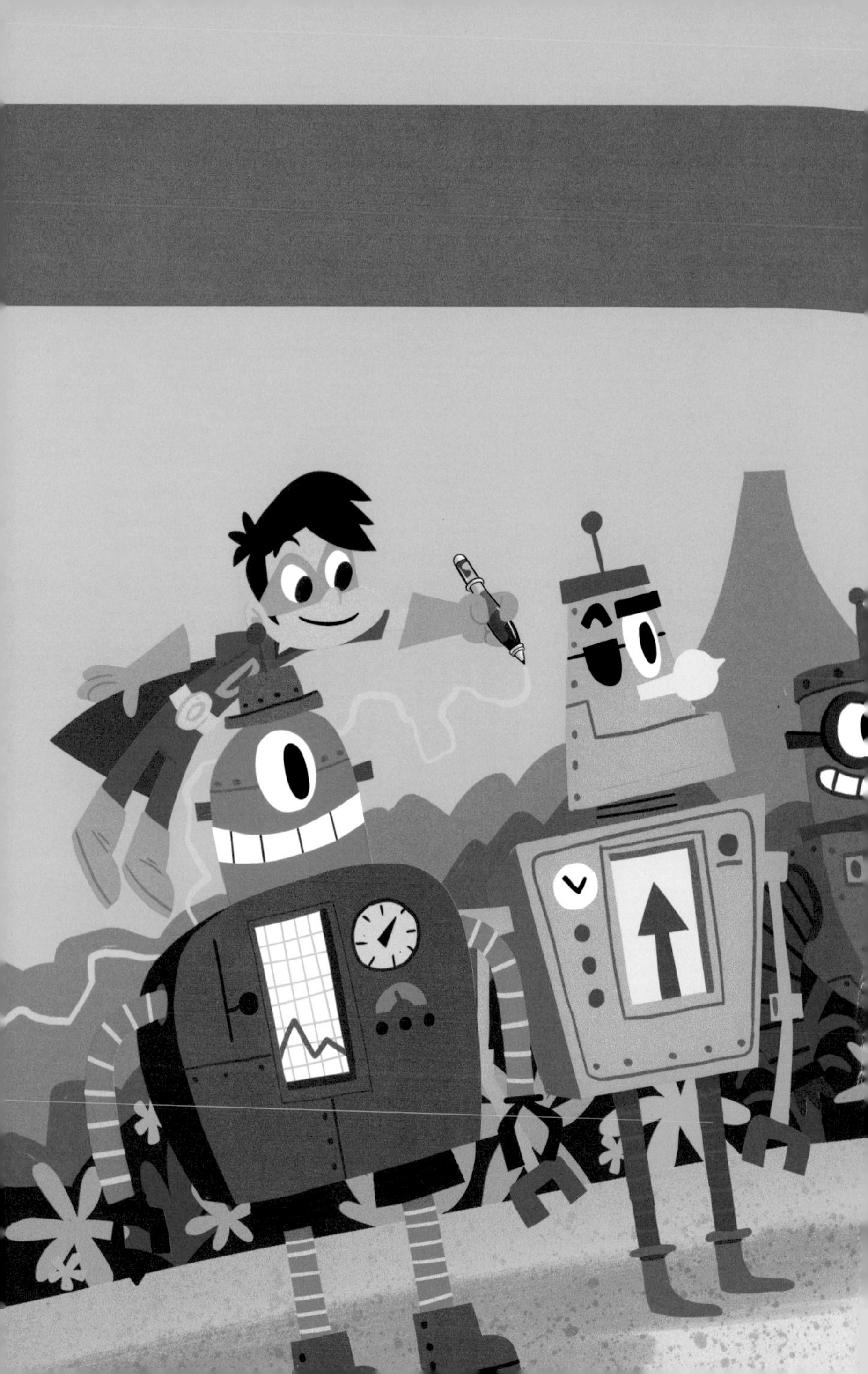

COOL SCHOOL

DREW PENDOUS #4

ESCAPES FROM Treasure Island

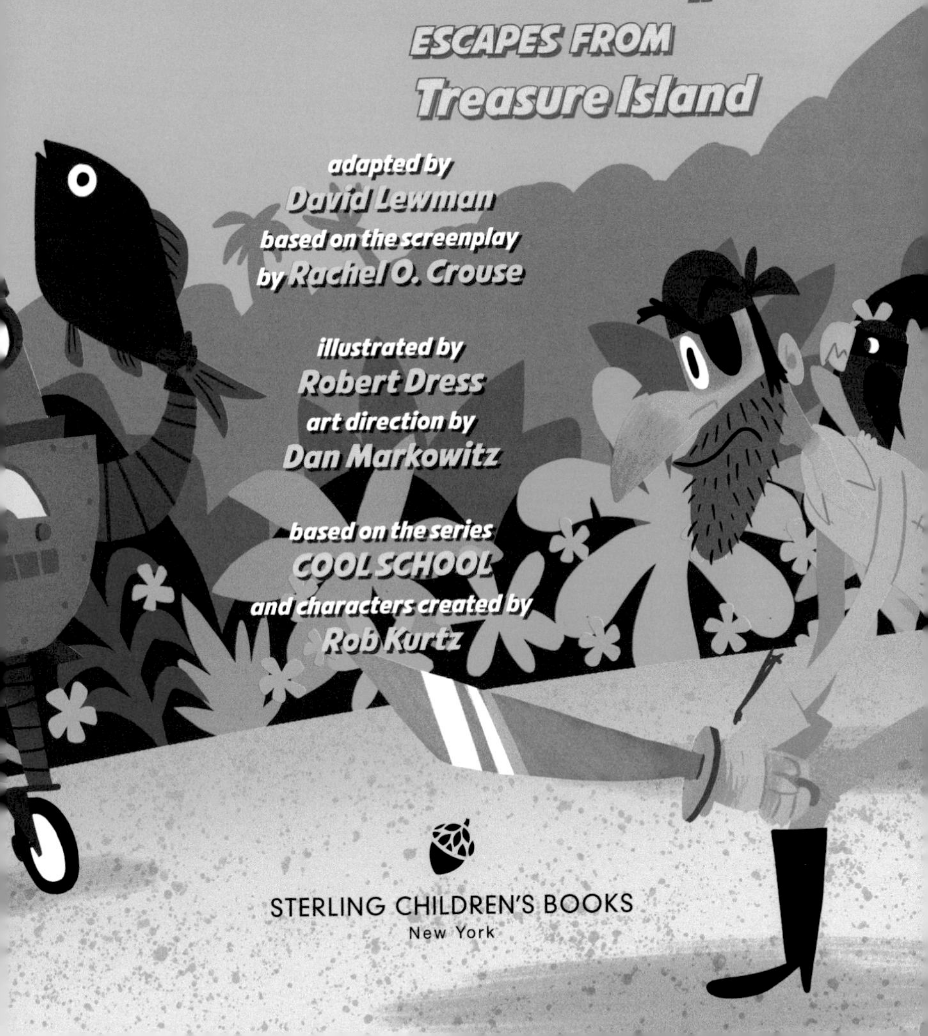

adapted by
David Lewman
based on the screenplay
by Rachel O. Crouse

illustrated by
Robert Dress
art direction by
Dan Markowitz

based on the series
COOL SCHOOL
and characters created by
Rob Kurtz

STERLING CHILDREN'S BOOKS
New York

STERLING CHILDREN'S BOOKS
New York

An Imprint of Sterling Publishing Co., Inc.
1166 Avenue of the Americas
New York, NY 10036

ISBN 978-1-4549-3108-9

Library of Congress Cataloging-in-Publication Data

Names: Lewman, David, adapter. | Dress, Robert, illustrator.
Title: Drew Pendous escapes from Treasure Island / adapted by David Lewman ; illustrated by Robert Dress.
Other titles: Based on: Cool School (Video series)
Description: New York, NY : Sterling Children's Books, [2020] | Series: Drew Pendous ; #4 | "Based on the screenplay by Rachel O. Crouse; based on the series Cool School and charcters created by Rob Kurtz."
Identifiers: LCCN 2019019224 | ISBN 9781454931089 (paperback)
Subjects: LCSH: Graphic novels. | BISAC: JUVENILE FICTION / Comics & Graphic Novels / Media Tie-In. | JUVENILE FICTION / Comics & Graphic Novels / General. | JUVENILE FICTION / Social Issues / Friendship.
Classification: LCC PZ7.7.L495 Drb 2019 | DDC 741.5/973--dc23 2019019224

Distributed in Canada by Sterling Publishing Co., Inc.
c/o Canadian Manda Group, 664 Annette Street
Toronto, Ontario M6S 2C8, Canada
Distributed in the United Kingdom by GMC Distribution Services
Castle Place, 166 High Street, Lewes, East Sussex BN7 1XU, England
Distributed in Australia by NewSouth Books
University of New South Wales, Sydney, NSW 2052, Australia

For information about custom editions, special sales, and premium and corporate purchases, please contact Sterling Special Sales at 800-805-5489 or specialsales@sterlingpublishing.com.

Manufactured in China

Lot #:
2 4 6 8 10 9 7 5 3 1
11/19

sterlingpublishing.com

CONTENTS

CHAPTER ONE

YES, it's time for another ***amazing adventure*** starring everyone's favorite superhero . . .

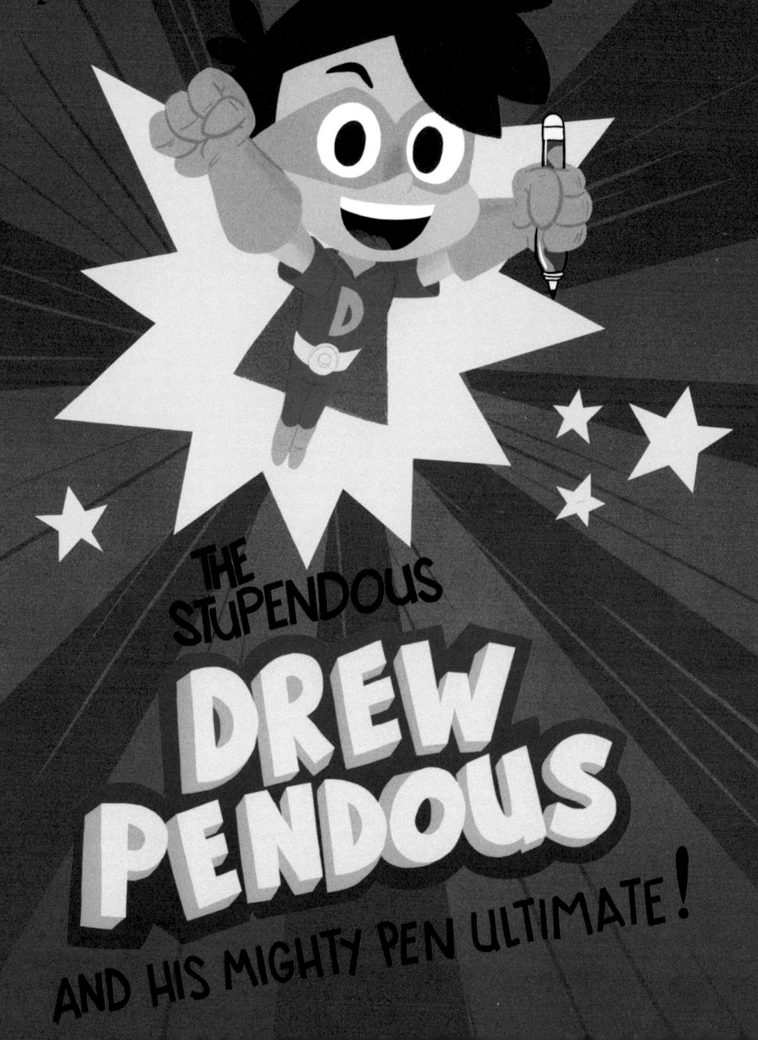
THE STUPENDOUS
DREW PENDOUS
AND HIS MIGHTY PEN ULTIMATE!

Drew ran down the hallway to the Cool School library. He couldn't wait for today's story, as told by the greatest storyteller ever, Ms. Booksy!

When he burst through the library doors, Drew called out, "Hi, Ms. Booksy!

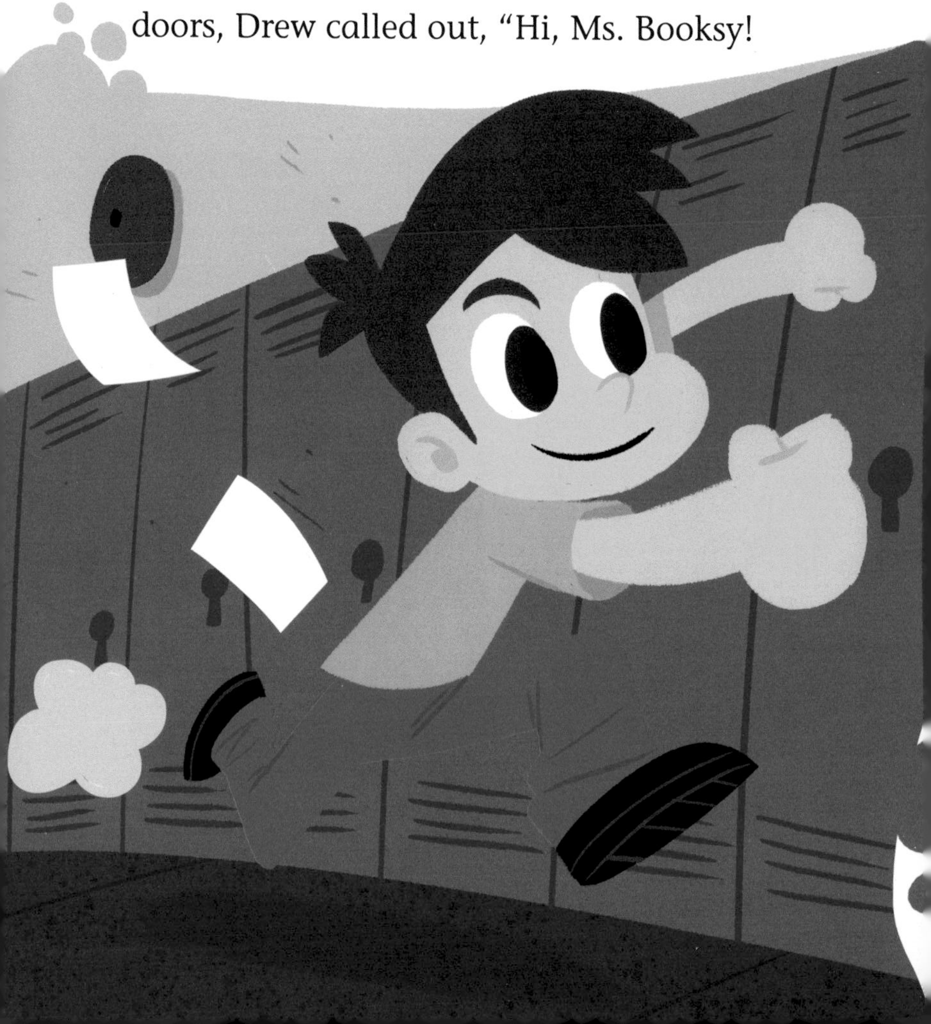

What **exciting story**  are we going to read today?" At some schools, you had to be really quiet when you went in the library, but at **Cool School**, talking out loud was okay. It was the coolest school ever!

"Oh, hi, Drew!" Ms. Booksy said.

She turned back to a shelf full of books. "I was just picking out today's book. There are so many good ones!" Ms. Booksy ran her finger along the spines of the books, reading the titles to herself. "No . . . not today . . . we just read this one . . . maybe next week . . ." she murmured as she considered which book to read. Suddenly, she stopped running her fingers along the books and pulled a red volume off the top shelf. "Oh!" she said. "Here's a good one!"

"What's it called?" Drew asked.

"*Treasure Island*," Ms. Booksy answered.

"*Treasure Island*," Drew repeated. "Sounds good! What's it about? ***An island made out of treasure?"***

"Well," Ms. Booksy said, flipping through the pages, "*Treasure Island* is one of ***my favorite*** stories. It's all about pirates! ***It's a classic!"***

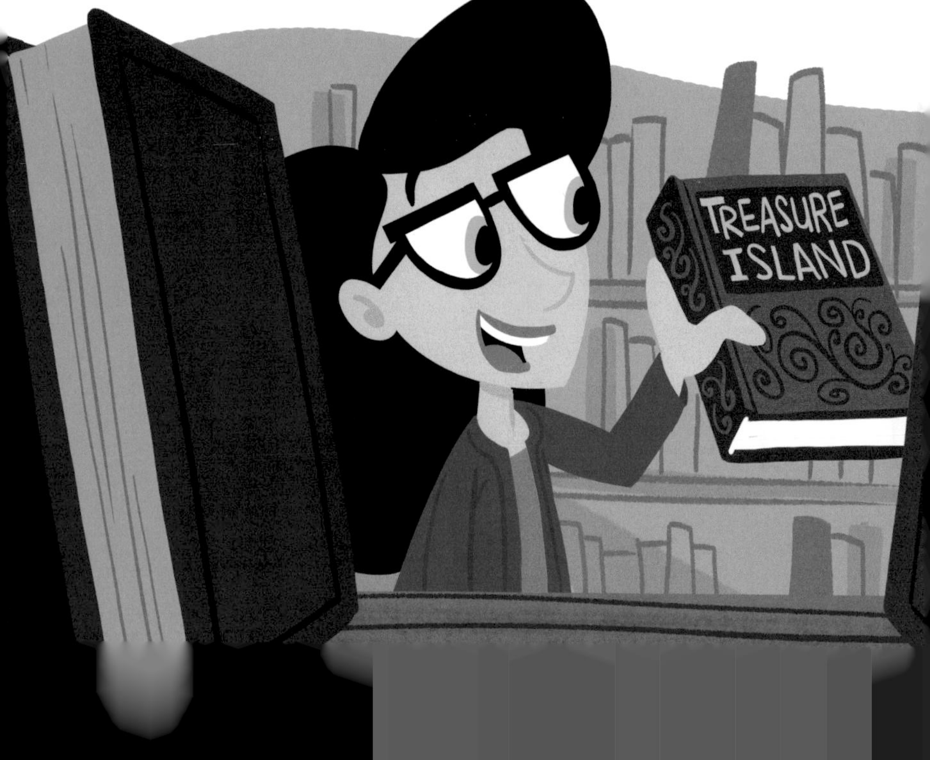
TREASURE
ISLAND

"Pirates?! Cool!" Drew exclaimed. "Everybody loves pirate stories!"

Ms. Booksy laughed. "That's good to hear! I like it when everybody loves the stories I read to them."

Drew looked around the library. "Hey, **where is everyone,** anyway? I'm not the only student in Cool School today, am I?"

"I don't think so," Ms. Booksy said, chuckling. "Oh, look! Here they come now!"

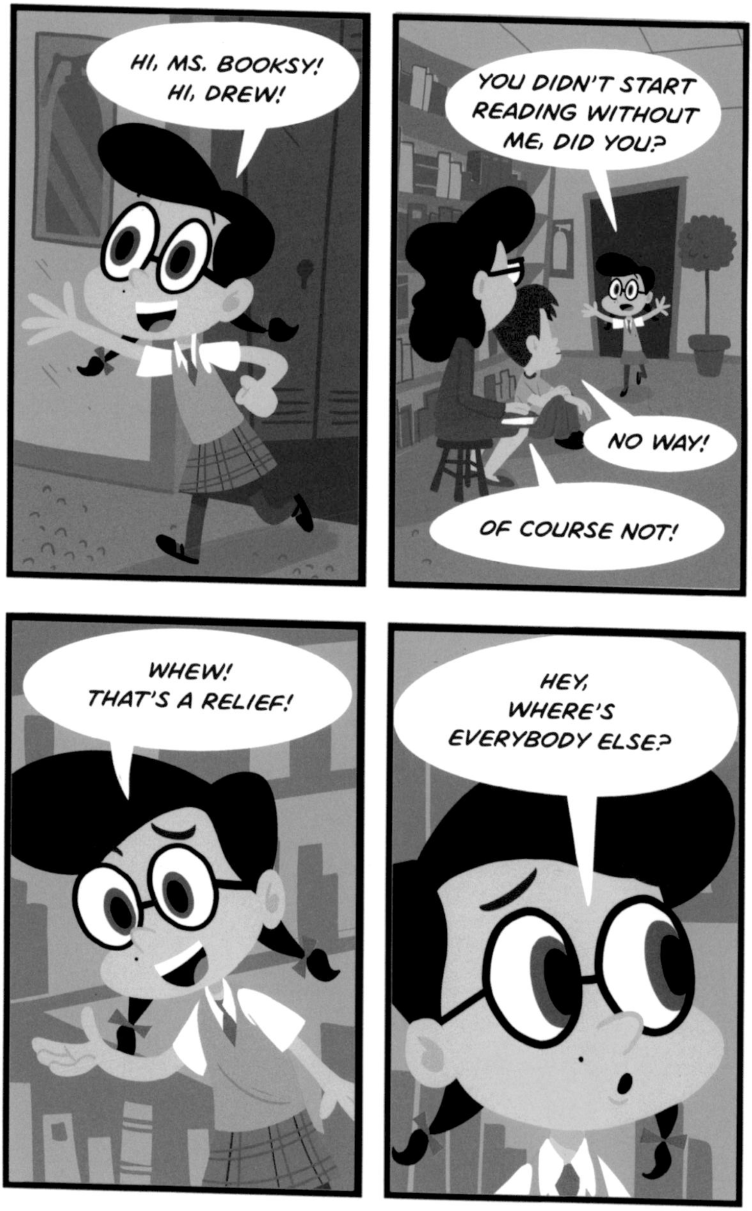
HI, MS. BOOKSY! HI, DREW!
YOU DIDN'T START READING WITHOUT ME, DID YOU?
NO WAY!
OF COURSE NOT!
WHEW! THAT'S A RELIEF!
HEY, WHERE'S EVERYBODY ELSE?

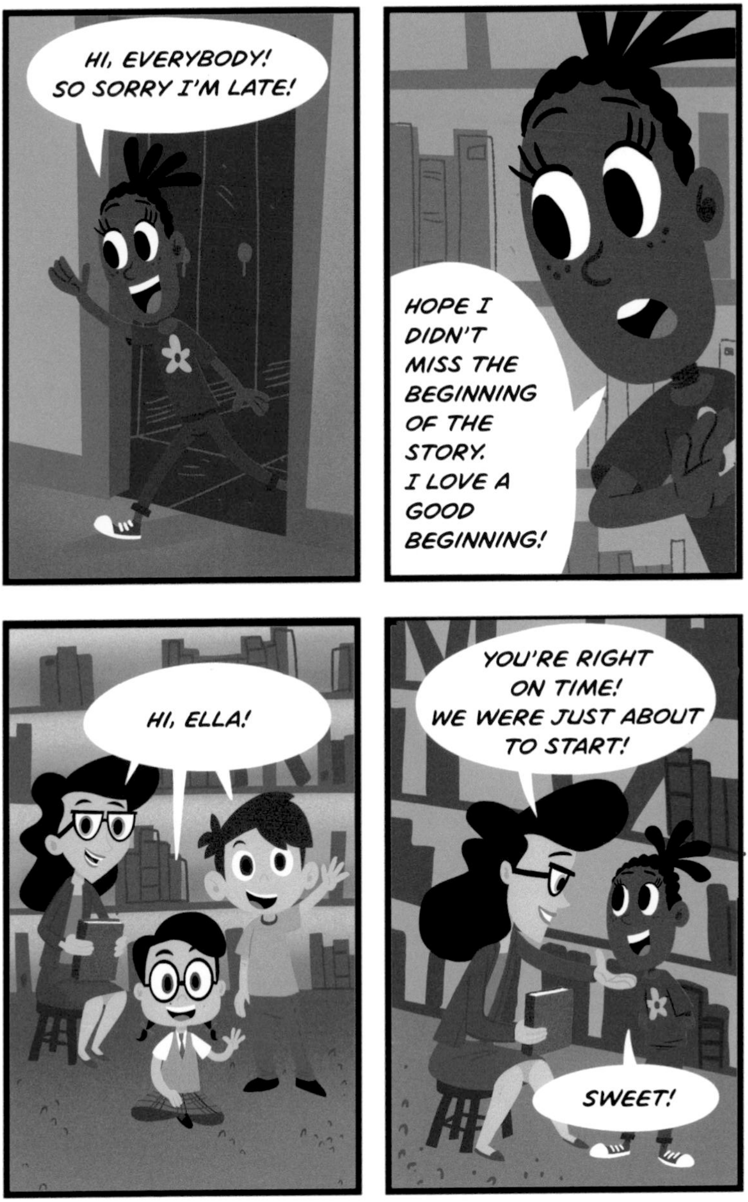
HI, EVERYBODY! SO SORRY I'M LATE!
HOPE I DIDN'T MISS THE BEGINNING OF THE STORY. I LOVE A GOOD BEGINNING!
HI, ELLA!
YOU'RE RIGHT ON TIME! WE WERE JUST ABOUT TO START!
SWEET!

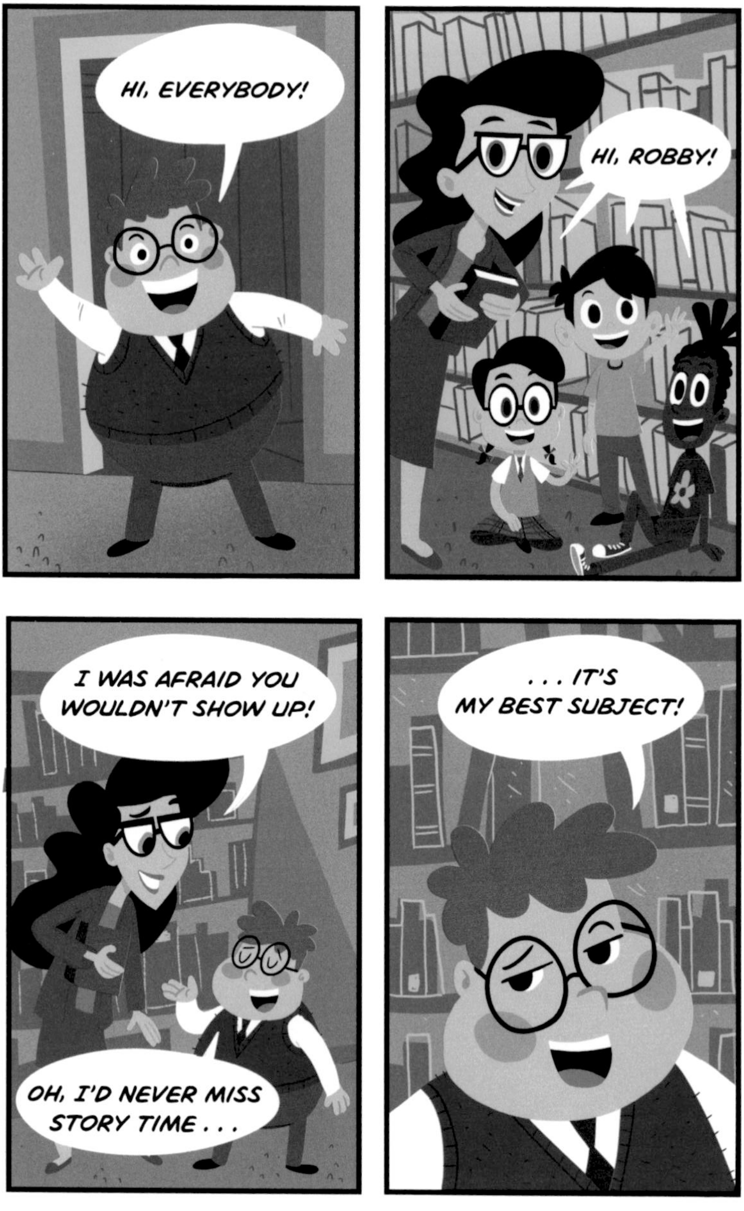
HI, EVERYBODY!
HI, ROBBY!
I WAS AFRAID YOU WOULDN'T SHOW UP!
OH, I'D NEVER MISS STORY TIME . . .
. . . IT'S MY BEST SUBJECT!

Other students poured into the library. They all sat down, waiting for Ms. Booksy to read *Treasure Island* to them.

"Ms. Booksy says this is a story about pirates!" Drew told everyone.

"Pirates?" Ella said. **"Cool!"**

"That's exactly what I said!" Drew exclaimed.

"It's also a story about hidden treasure!" Ms. Booksy explained.

"Hidden treasure?" Drew said. **"Awesome!"**

He imagined an old wooden chest full of gleaming gold coins. If he had a chest full of treasure, he could buy all kinds of things! Toys! Video games! Sports equipment! Books!

Ms. Booksy held up the book for everyone to see. "Okay," she said. "*Treasure Island*! **Here we go!"** She closed her eyes and wiggled her nose. Magical power glowed around her nose, and then . . .

. . . ***POOF!*** Ms. Booksy disappeared in a puff of smoke!

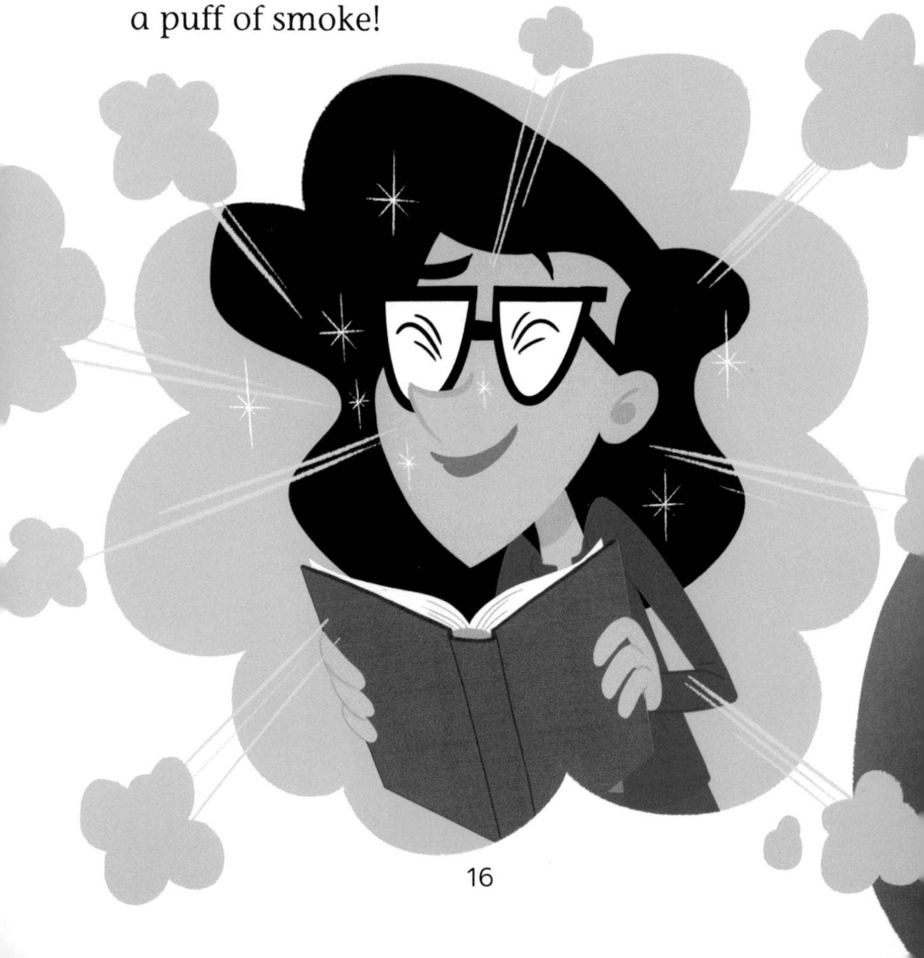

CHAPTER TWO

NOBODY was surprised. At an amazing school like Cool School, the storyteller *always* **magically disappeared** into the story she was telling.

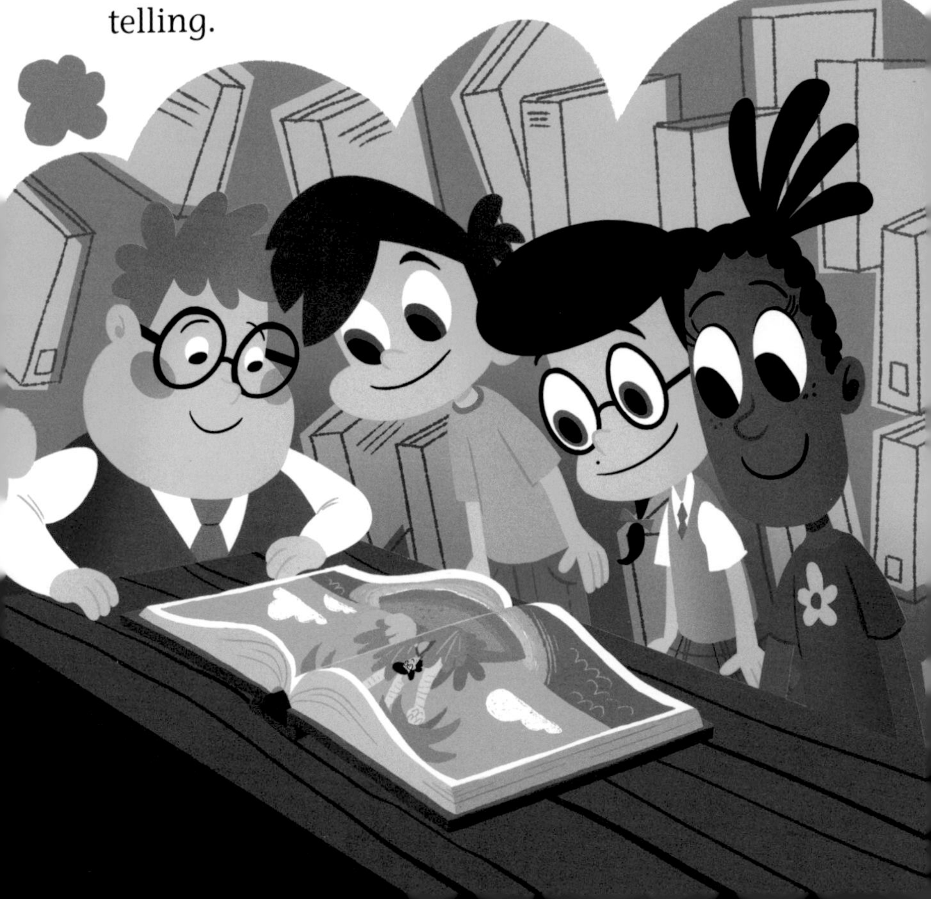

Drew got an idea. *I know what I'll do,* he thought to himself. *I'll go into the story with Ms. Booksy and find the hidden treasure!*

He'd watched Ms. Booksy very carefully to see just what she did to disappear into the story. **He planned to do exactly what she did.**

First, he closed his eyes. Then, he wiggled his nose just like Ms. Booksy did.

But when Drew opened his eyes, **he was NOT in the story** of *Treasure Island.* He was still sitting in the library,

exactly where he'd been before he wiggled his nose! *It didn't work!* he thought to himself, disappointed. *Ms. Booksy must have a magic nose wiggle!*

Ella had noticed Drew closing his eyes and wiggling his nose. **"Nice try, Drew!"** she said, giggling. "But only Ms. Booksy can disappear into the story!"

"Oh, right," Drew said innocently. "I was just kidding around."

"Good one," Ella said.

Drew guessed it made sense. Teachers had special powers beyond those of mere human beings.

But how was he supposed to **find the hidden treasure** if he couldn't magically follow Ms. Booksy into the story? There *had to be* some other way!

While he was trying to think of another way into the story, Drew absentmindedly tapped his mighty Pen Ultimate against his knee. He noticed what he was doing, and got a brilliant idea!

I know! he thought. *I'll just use my mighty Pen Ultimate to DRAW myself into the story!*

First, Drew used his mighty Pen Ultimate to draw a big orange "D" on his shirt. Thanks to the magical powers of his **Pen Ultimate,** he instantly changed into his superhero costume! His boots, gloves, and mask matched the "D" on his shirt. His pants and shirt were blue. He had a yellow belt with a big buckle and a red cape. ***He was ready for action!***

"Hey, Drew!" Robbie said. "Are you about to do some exciting superhero stuff?"

"I sure am!" Drew agreed.

"I knew it!" Robbie said. "Go get 'em!"

"Thanks, Robbie!" Drew said. ***"I'm on my way!"***

Next, Drew used his mighty Pen Ultimate to draw a picture of himself in

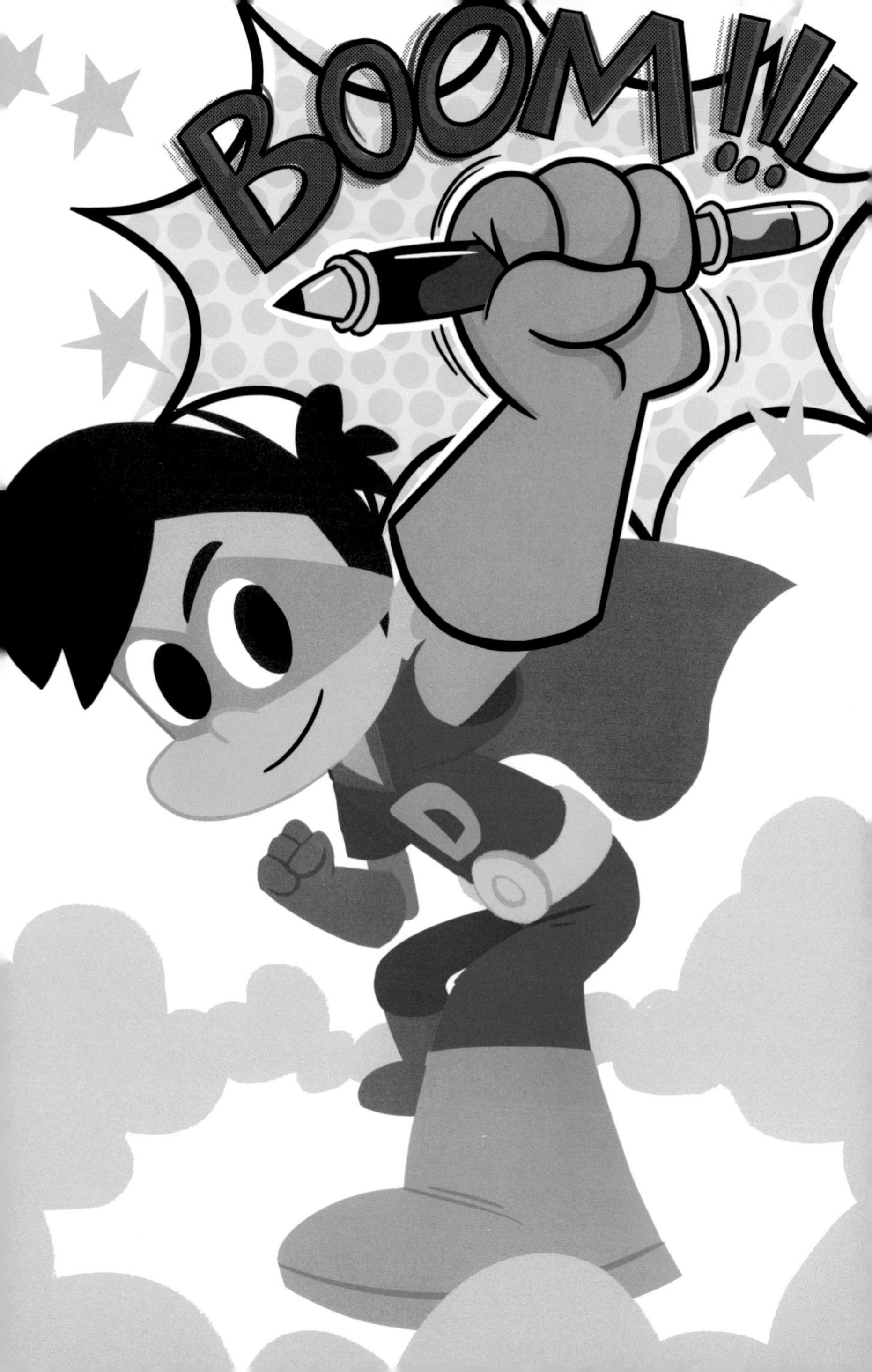
BOOM!!!

his superhero outfit next to Ms. Booksy. He knew he wasn't supposed to draw in a library book, but he thought this was an emergency! He really wanted to help Ms. Booksy **find that treasure!** When he came back, he'd make sure to erase his drawing from *Treasure Island*.

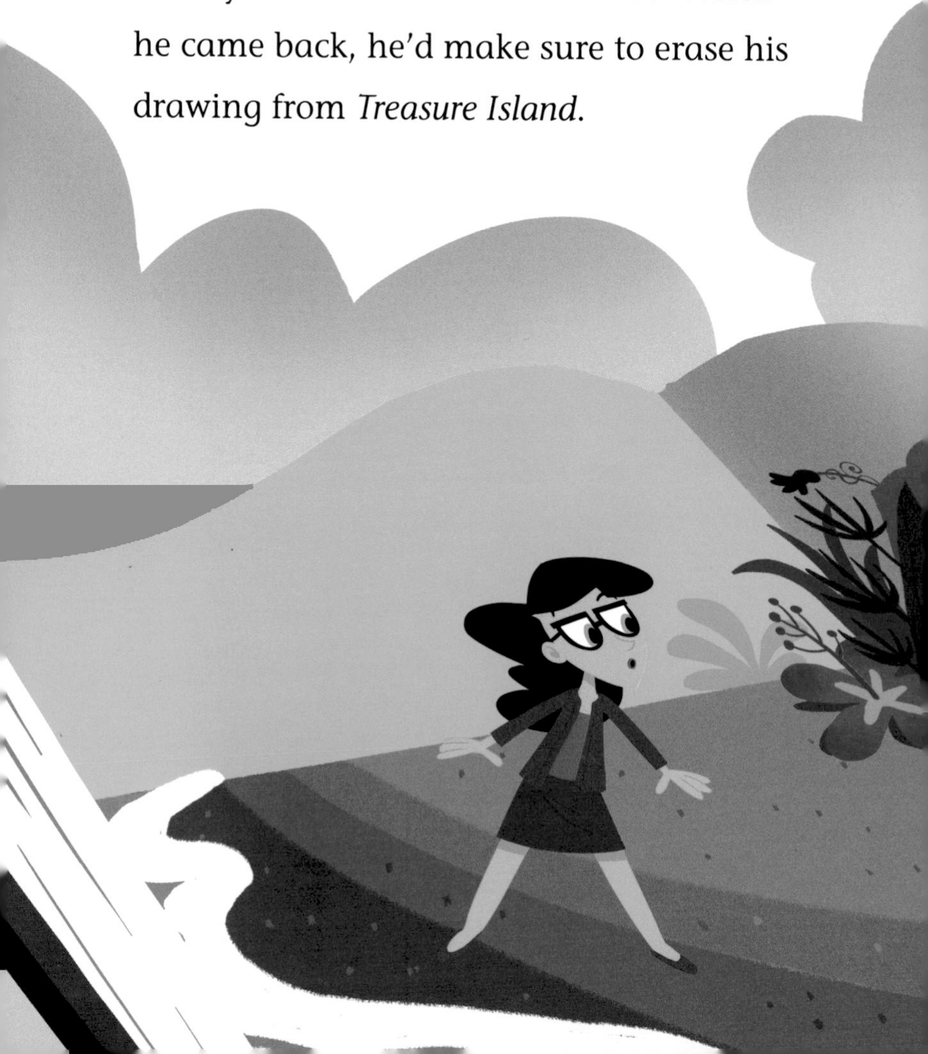

He studied his drawing. *Not bad,* he thought. *Anyone who saw that picture would know it was me. Especially since I'm the only kid at Cool School who wears a cape and a shirt with a big 'D' on it.*

Drew closed his eyes. Then he **wiggled his nose,** and . . .

. . . POOF! Drew disappeared in a puff of smoke!

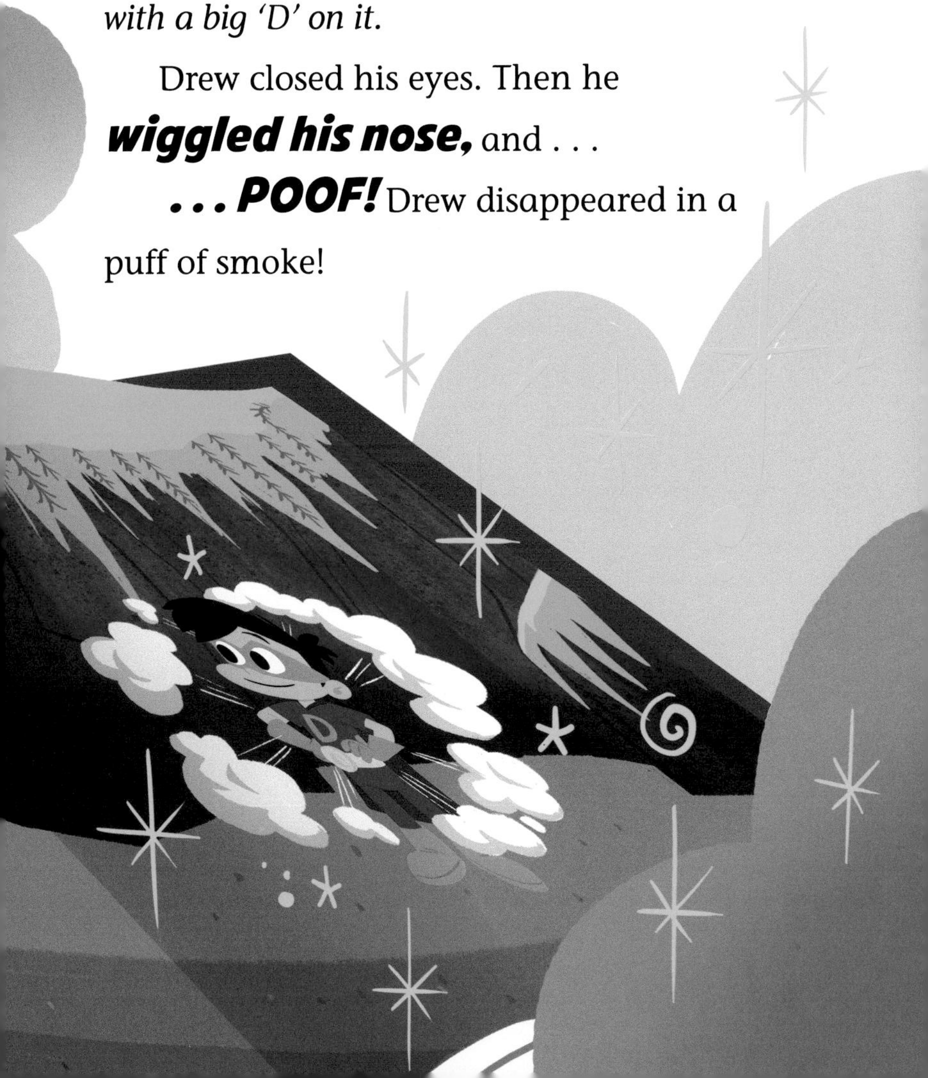

CHAPTER THREE

MS. BOOKSY was standing on a sandy beach at the edge of a tropical island. Lots of colorful plants grew nearby: bushes with purple leaves, trees with pink leaves, and palm trees with brown coconuts. A little red crab waved its claws in the warm air.

"Once upon a time," she said, beginning to tell her story, "there was a place called *Treasure Island—*"

POOF! Suddenly Drew Pendous appeared right next to her on the beach!

"Awesome!" he said. "My drawing—and my nose-wiggling—totally worked! I'm in the story with Ms. Booksy!"

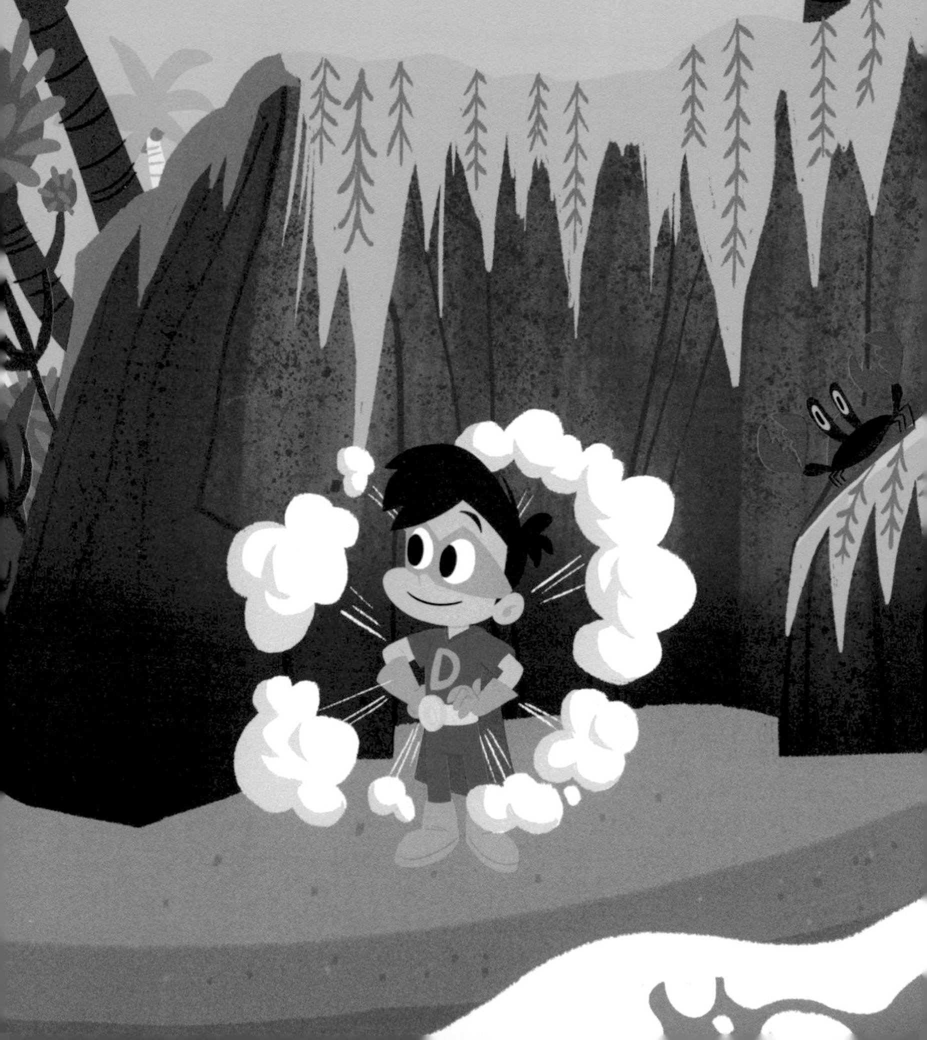

"Drew!" Ms. Booksy cried, surprised to see him. ***"What are you doing here?***

Drew put his fists on his hips, striking his best superhero pose. (He'd seen it in a comic book.) "I want to help you ***fight the pirates*** and then ***find the treasure!"***

Ms. Booksy considered this. She guessed it would be all right for Drew to come along. "Well, okay," she said. ***"You can be the cabin boy."***

Drew wasn't exactly sure what a cabin boy was, or what his duties consisted of, but it sounded all right to him. ***"Cabin boy with the mighty Pen Ultimate, though . . . right?"***

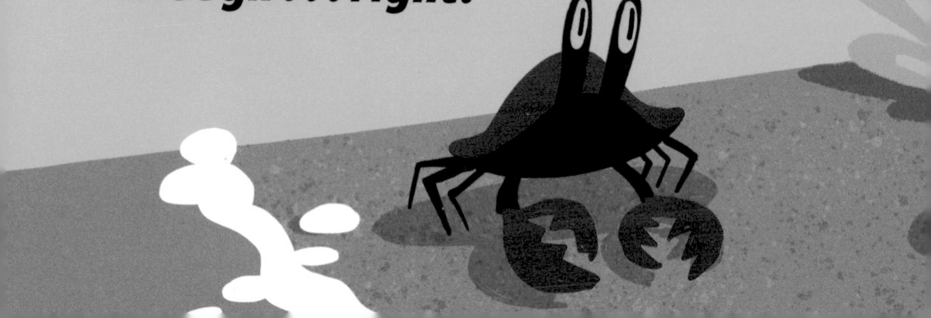

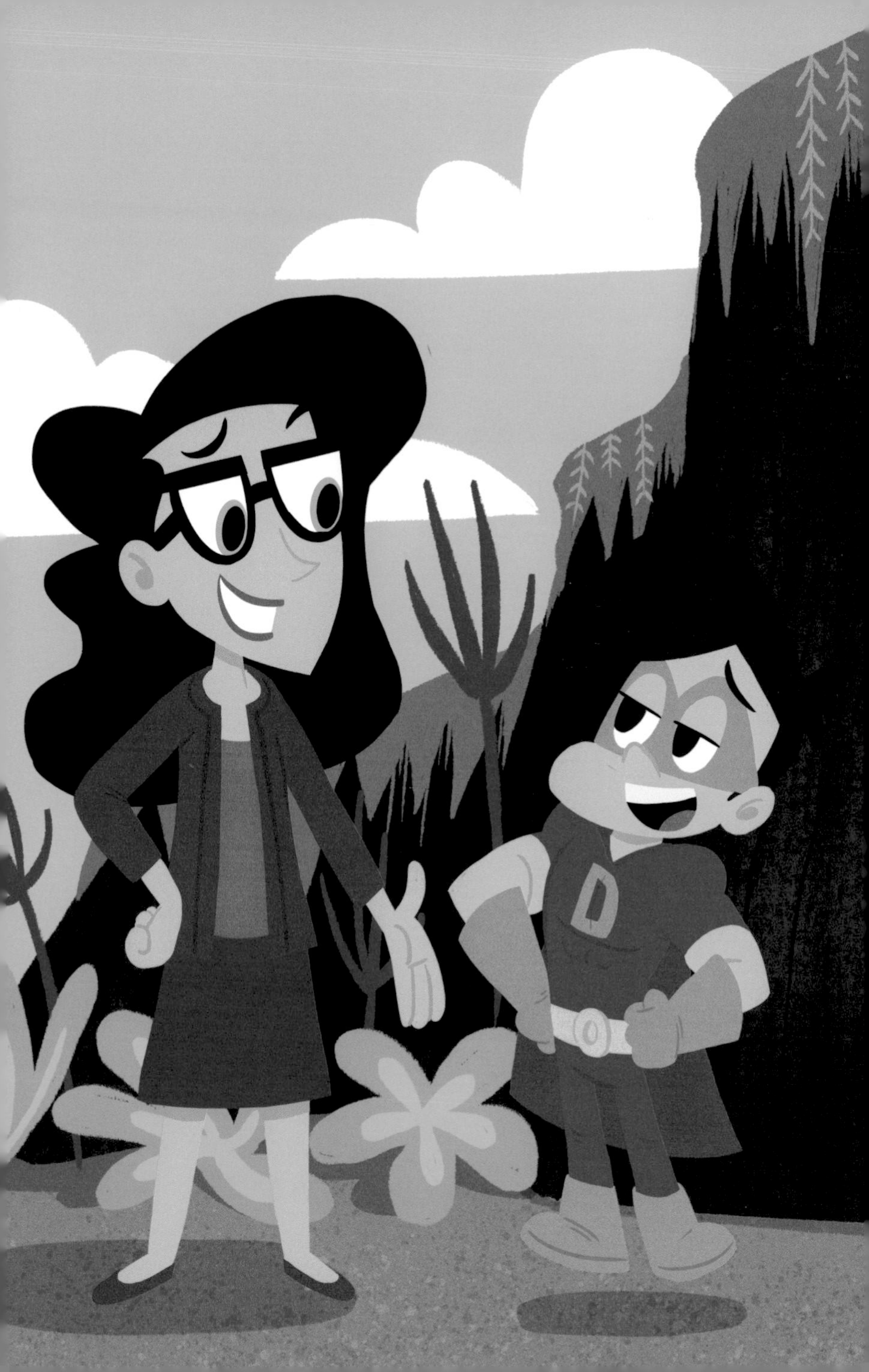

"Of course," Ms. Booksy agreed, nodding. "All right, I guess you'll have to come along on this **adventure** then!"

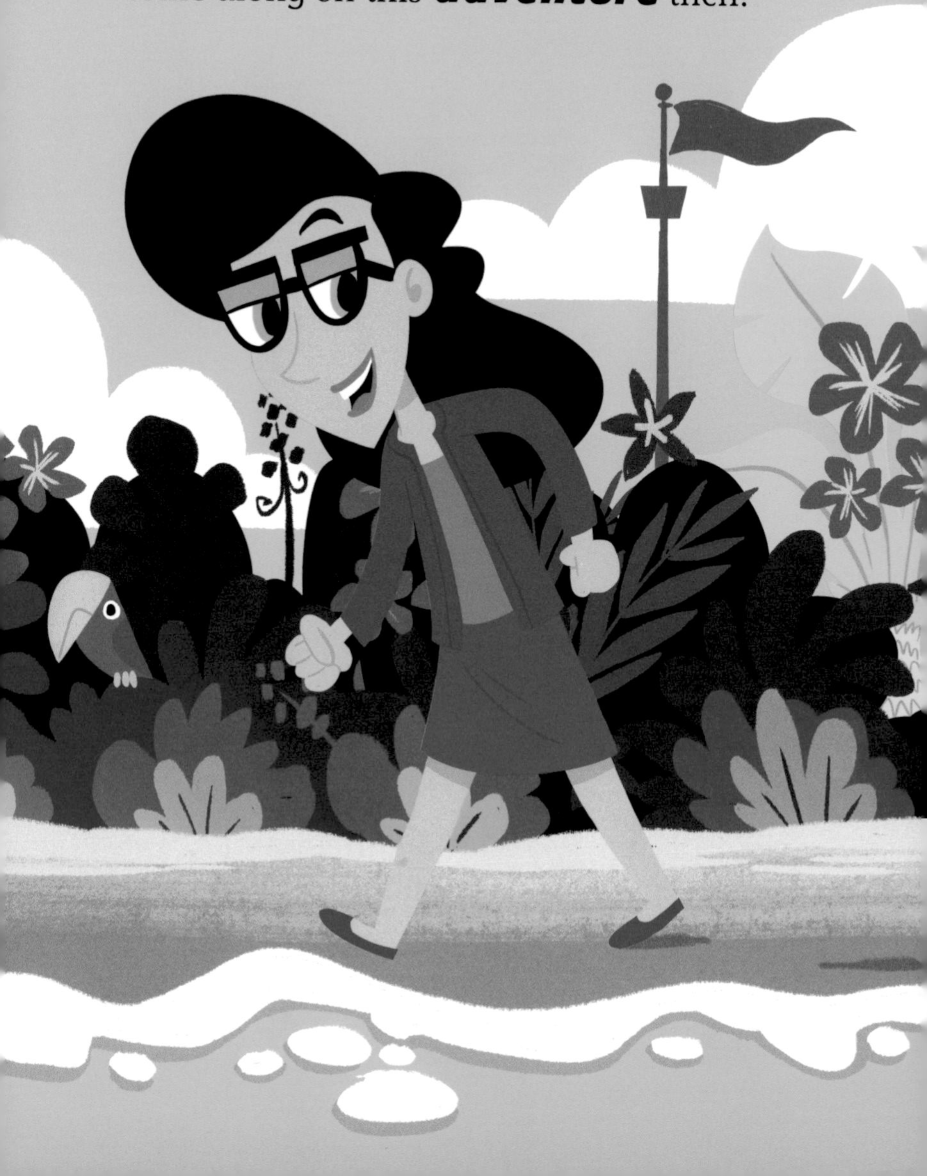

The two of them started walking along the beach, leaving their footprints in the white sand. Drew kept a constant lookout for treasure . . .

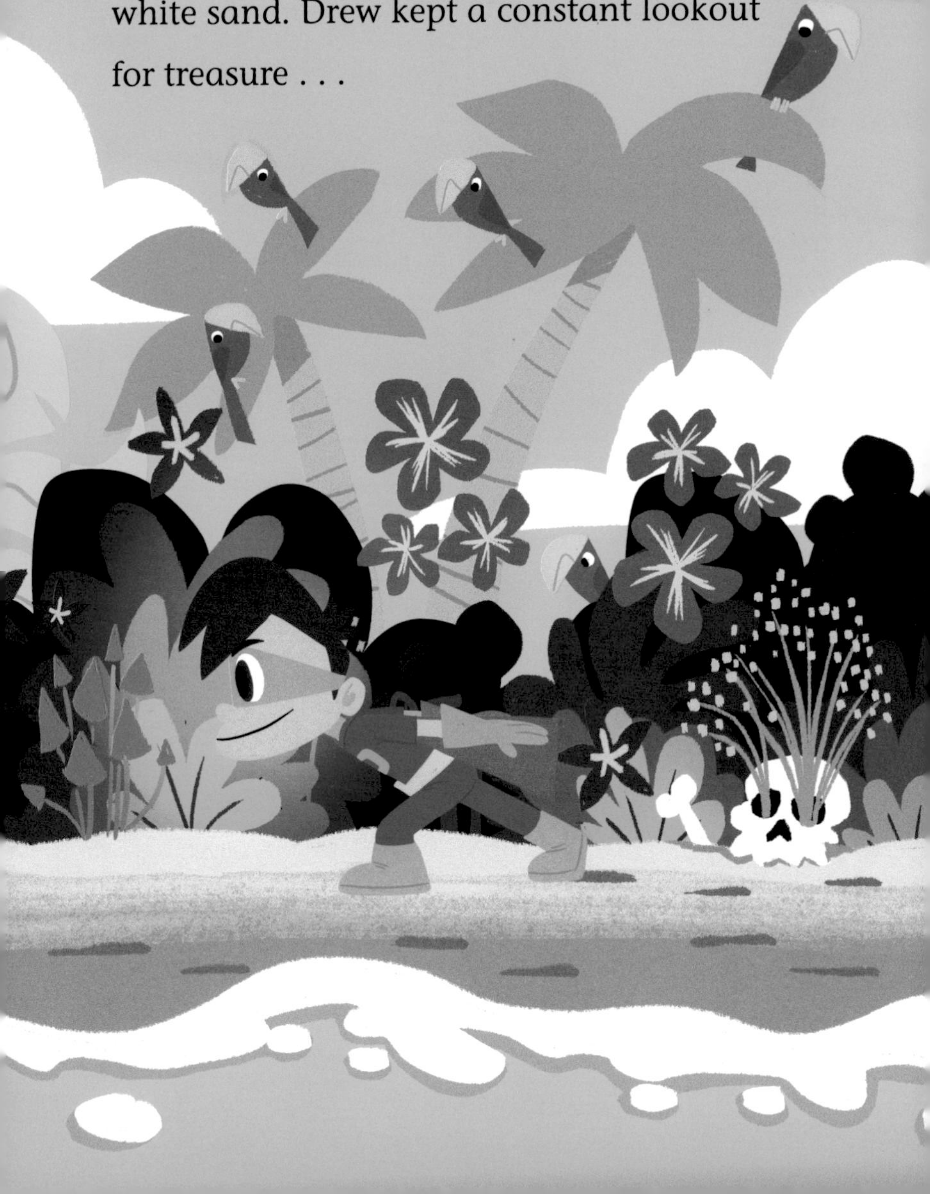

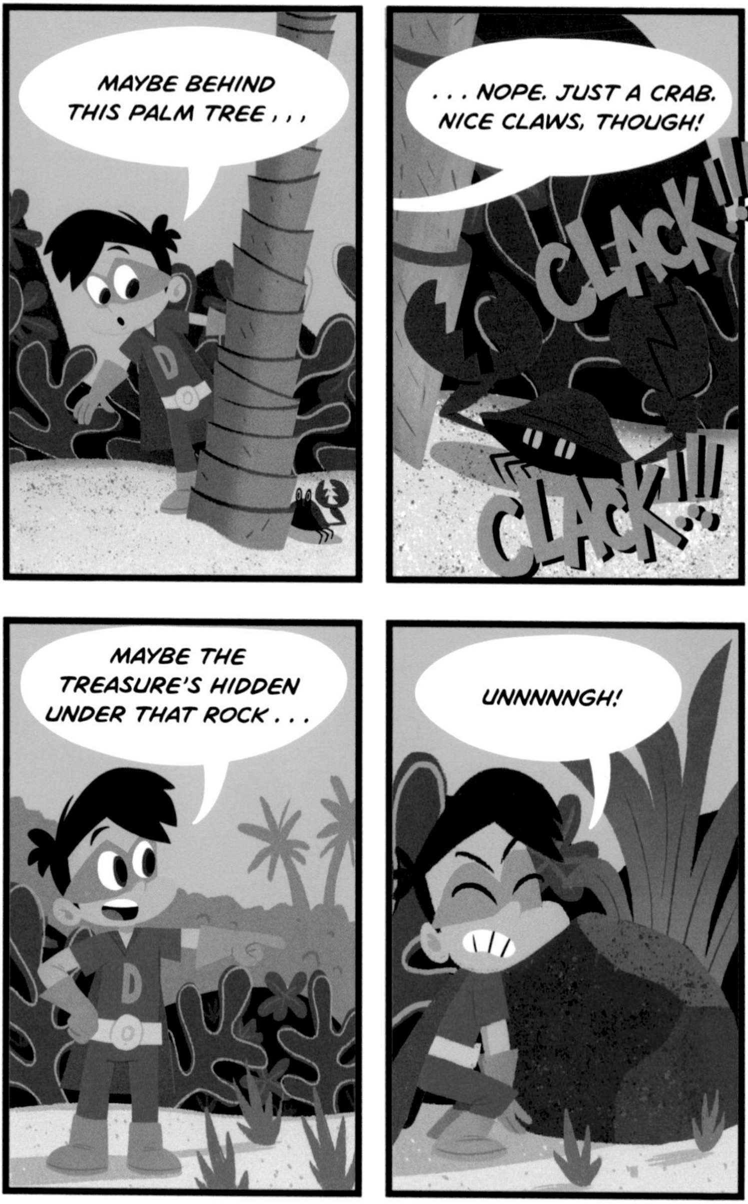
MAYBE BEHIND THIS PALM TREE . . .
. . . NOPE. JUST A CRAB. NICE CLAWS, THOUGH!
CLACK!!!
CLACK!!!
MAYBE THE TREASURE'S HIDDEN UNDER THAT ROCK . . .
UNNNNNGH!

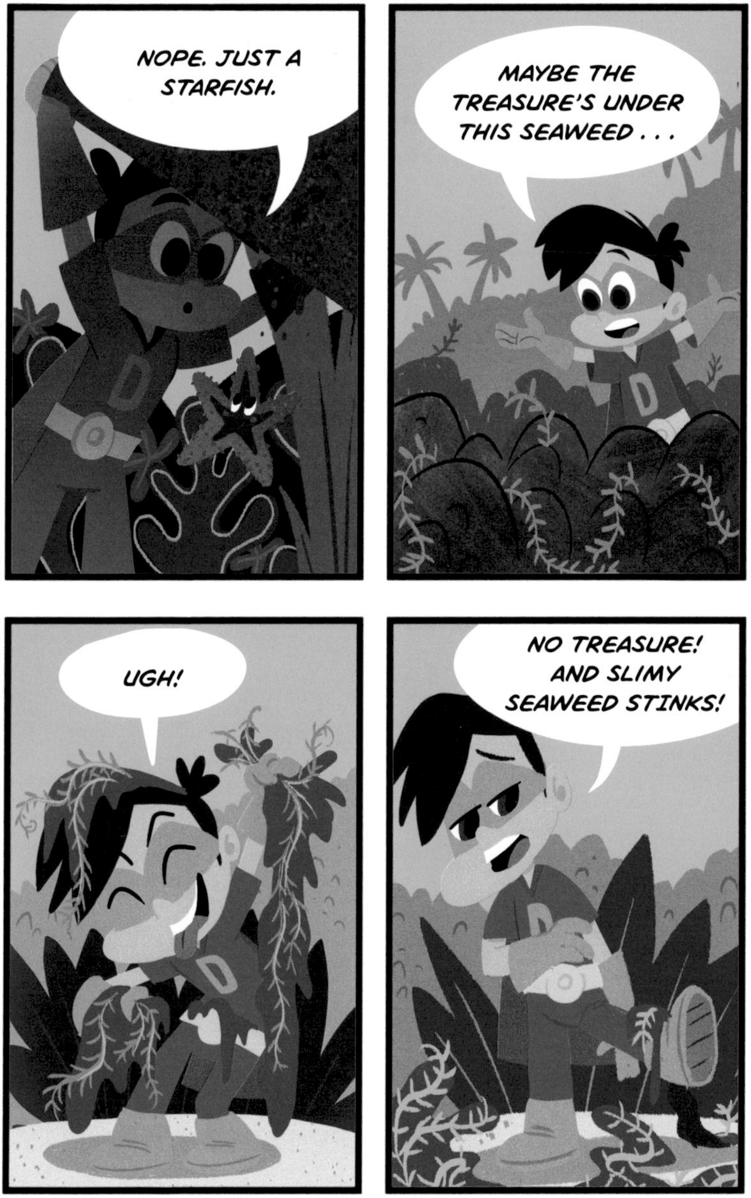
NOPE. JUST A STARFISH.
MAYBE THE TREASURE'S UNDER THIS SEAWEED . . .
UGH!
NO TREASURE! AND SLIMY SEAWEED STINKS!

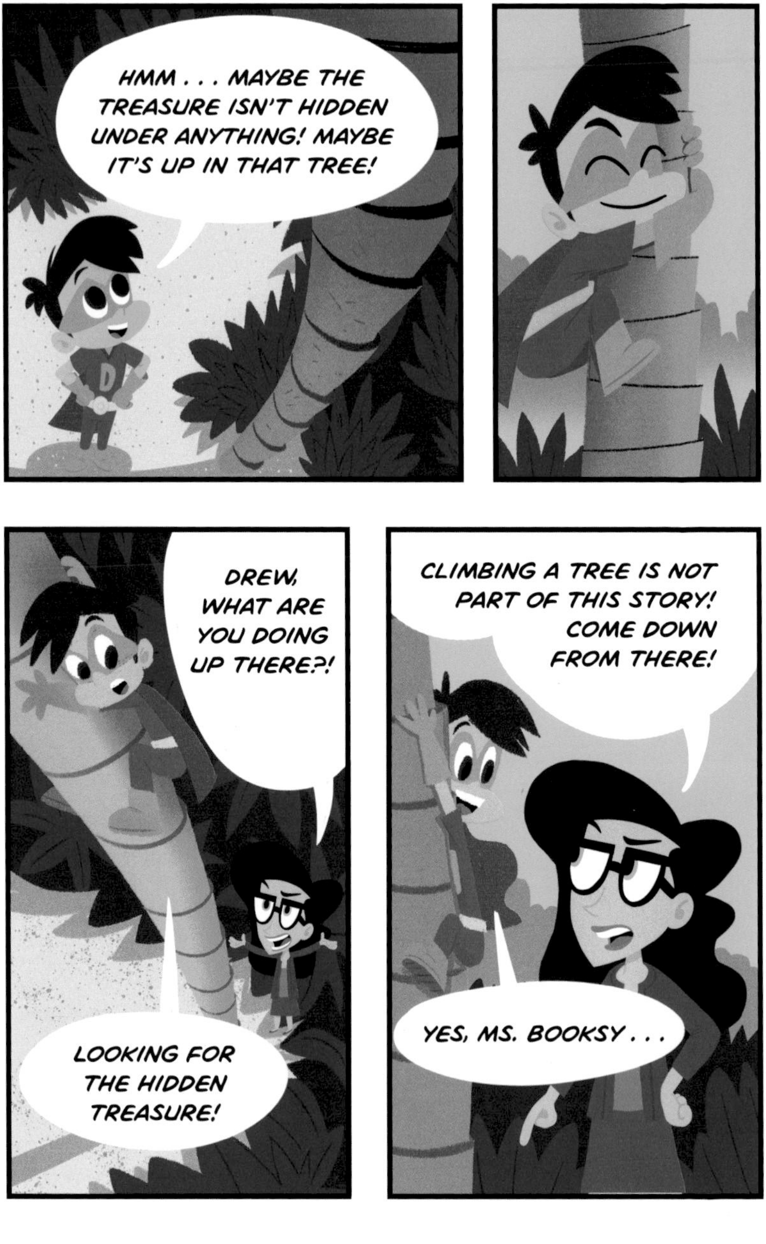
HMM . . . MAYBE THE TREASURE ISN'T HIDDEN UNDER ANYTHING! MAYBE IT'S UP IN THAT TREE!
DREW, WHAT ARE YOU DOING UP THERE?!
LOOKING FOR THE HIDDEN TREASURE!
CLIMBING A TREE IS NOT PART OF THIS STORY! COME DOWN FROM THERE!
YES, MS. BOOKSY . . .

"Now," Ms. Booksy said. "I'll continue with the story. Because this beautiful little island was called *Treasure Island*, lots of people were sure that there was a **chest full of treasure** hidden somewhere on the island."

"Lots of people," Drew agreed, "including me!"

"And including pirates!" Ms. Booksy continued. "No one loves treasure more than pirates, and a lot of the **world's scariest pirates** were convinced that there was a big wooden chest full of gold and jewels buried somewhere on Treasure Island."

They walked along the beach, and Ms. Booksy kept telling her story. "One sunny day, Drew and Ms. Booksy were strolling along the island's sandy beach, when out of nowhere—"

"THEY GOT TRAPPED INSIDE THE STORY!" interrupted a voice from above.

Ms. Booksy and Drew were shocked. **They looked all around**—even up in the sky—to see who had spoken, but they didn't see anyone at all!

"Drew," Ms. Booksy said nervously, "did that voice sound familiar to you?"

Drew nodded. "It sure did! To me, ***it sounded exactly like . . . CAPTAIN HOOKSY!***"

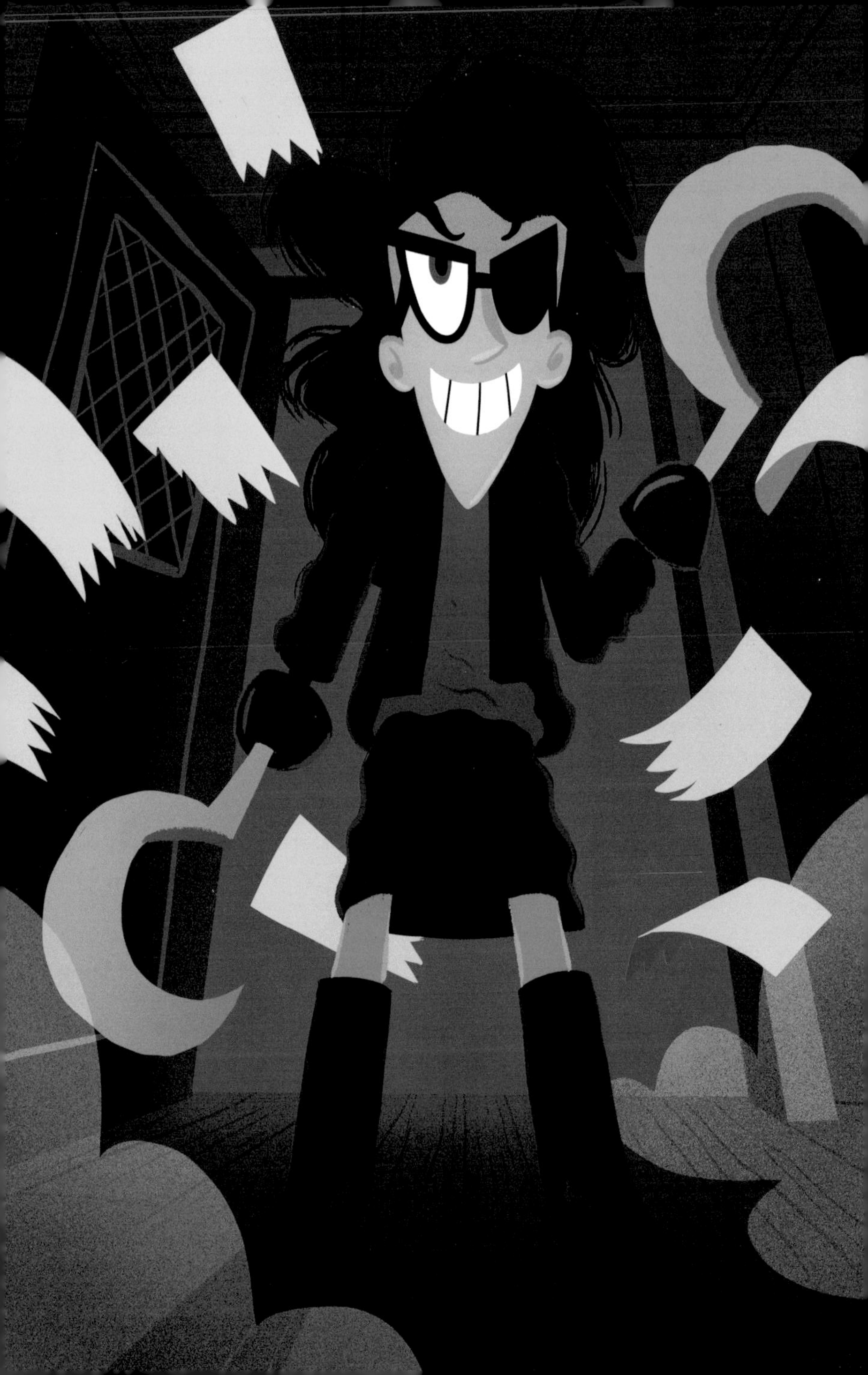

CHAPTER FOUR

DREW WAS RIGHT!

The mysterious voice belonged to Captain Hooksy, **the evil teacher at Cruel School!** Cruel School was the complete opposite of Cool School. All the teachers at Cruel School were mean instead of nice.

Captain Hooksy looked a lot like Ms. Booksy, but instead of green eyes, **she had red eyes!** And one of them was covered with a black eyepatch! **And** instead of hands, she had **sharp, wicked hooks!**

"Oh, no!" Drew cried. "Captain Hooksy must have sneaked into the Cool School library and taken your storybook!"

"Really?" Ms. Booksy said. **"That's a ROTTEN thing to do!"**

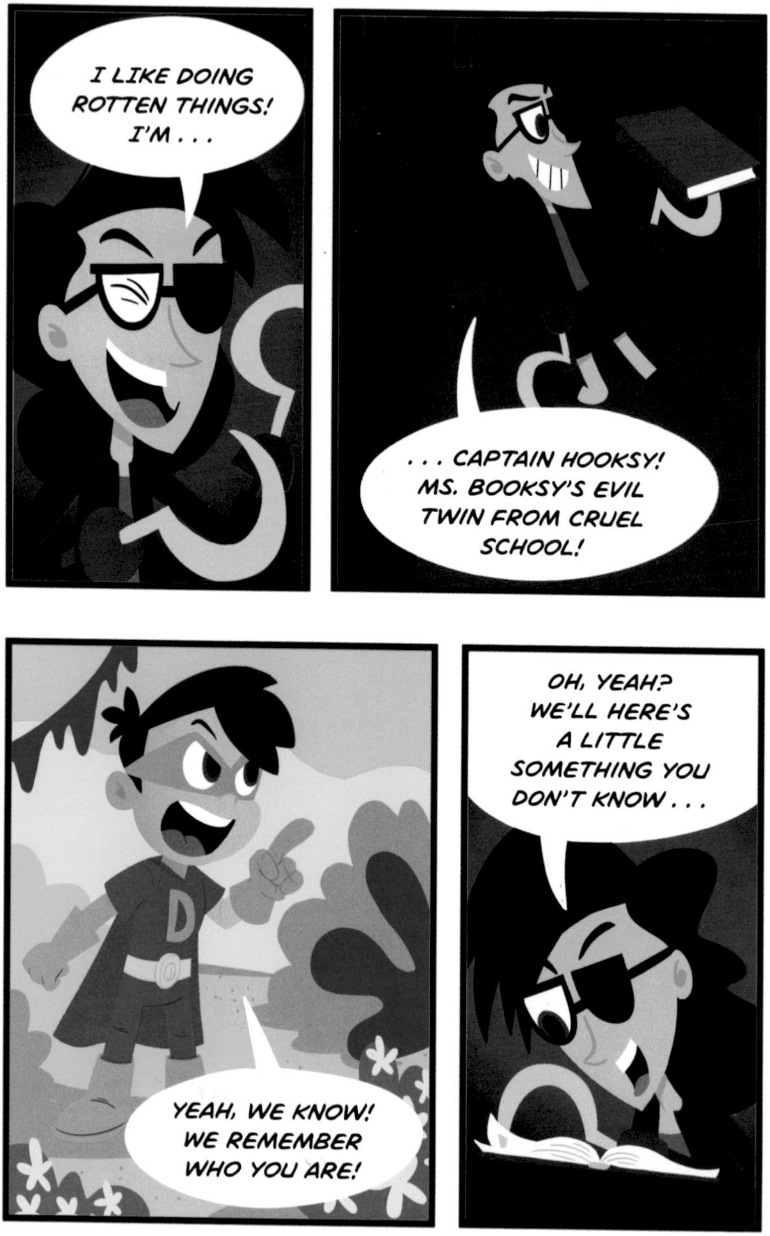
I LIKE DOING ROTTEN THINGS! I'M . . .
. . . CAPTAIN HOOKSY! MS. BOOKSY'S EVIL TWIN FROM CRUEL SCHOOL!
YEAH, WE KNOW! WE REMEMBER WHO YOU ARE!
OH, YEAH? WE'LL HERE'S A LITTLE SOMETHING YOU DON'T KNOW . . .

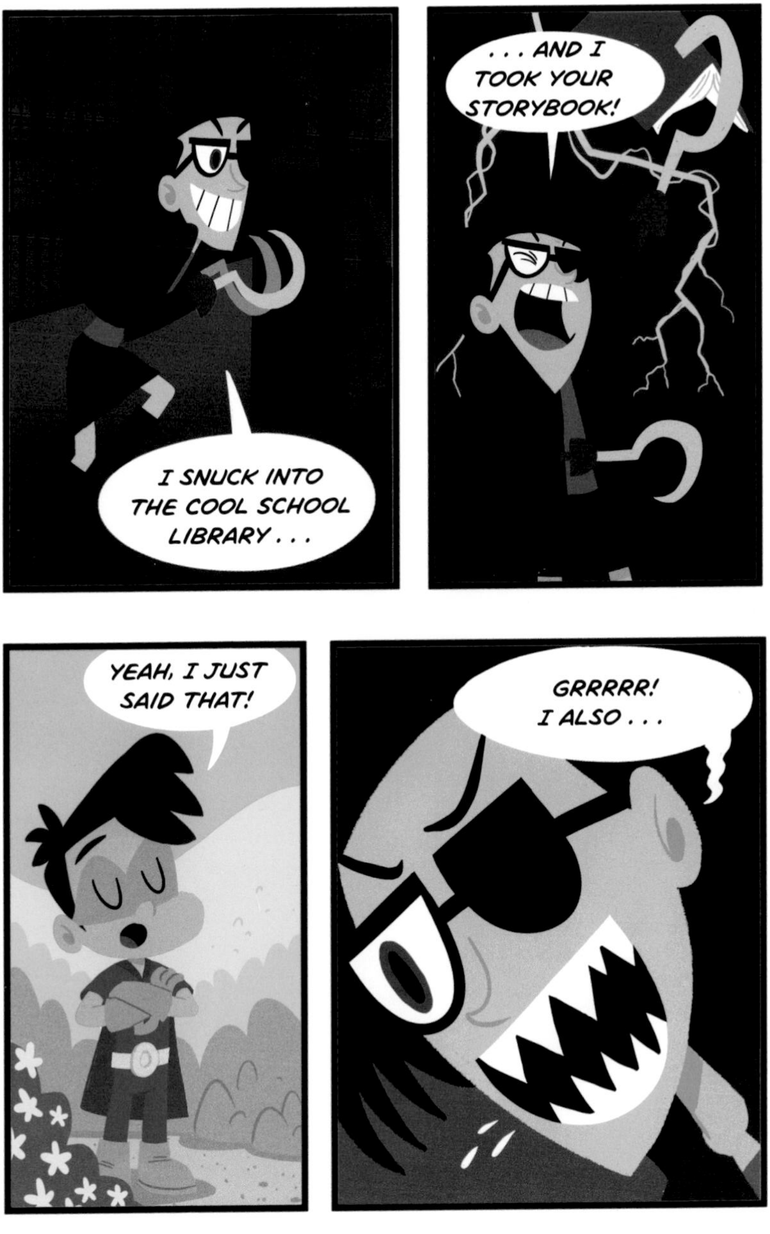
I SNUCK INTO THE COOL SCHOOL LIBRARY . . .
. . . AND I TOOK YOUR STORYBOOK!
YEAH, I JUST SAID THAT!
GRRRRR! I ALSO . . .

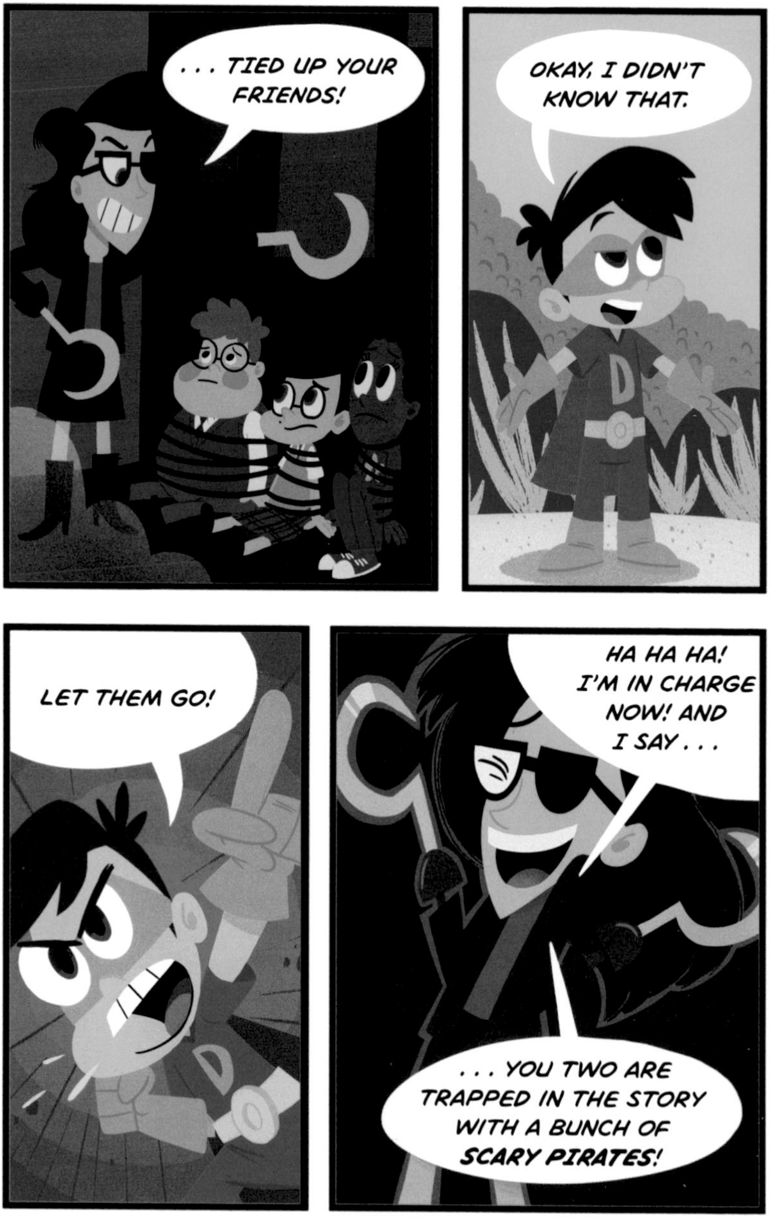
. . . TIED UP YOUR FRIENDS!
OKAY, I DIDN'T KNOW THAT.
LET THEM GO!
HA HA HA! I'M IN CHARGE NOW! AND I SAY . . .
. . . YOU TWO ARE TRAPPED IN THE STORY WITH A BUNCH OF SCARY PIRATES!

Drew was confused. "Scary pirates? I don't see any scary pirates!"

POOF! A gang of scary pirates appeared right next to Drew and Ms. Booksy! As long as Captain Hooksy held the storybook, whatever she said came true!

"Never mind," Drew said, correcting himself. **"I see them!"**

A tall, skinny pirate with an **eyepatch**, a **peg leg**, and a **red parrot** on his shoulder stepped forward, holding up a long, sharp sword. "*Ahhrrr,*" he growled. "I'm **Long John Silver,** the scariest pirate in the world!"

"*Squawk*! **Scariest pirate** in the world!" the parrot echoed.

Drew put on a brave face. ***"I'm Drew Pendous, and I'm here to defeat you!"***

"Eat you! Eat you!" squawked the parrot.

"No," Drew corrected, "*defeat* you!"

"Excuse me," Ms. Booksy said, "but I tell the stories around here, and this is not how this story goes! ***You're going down***, pirate man!"

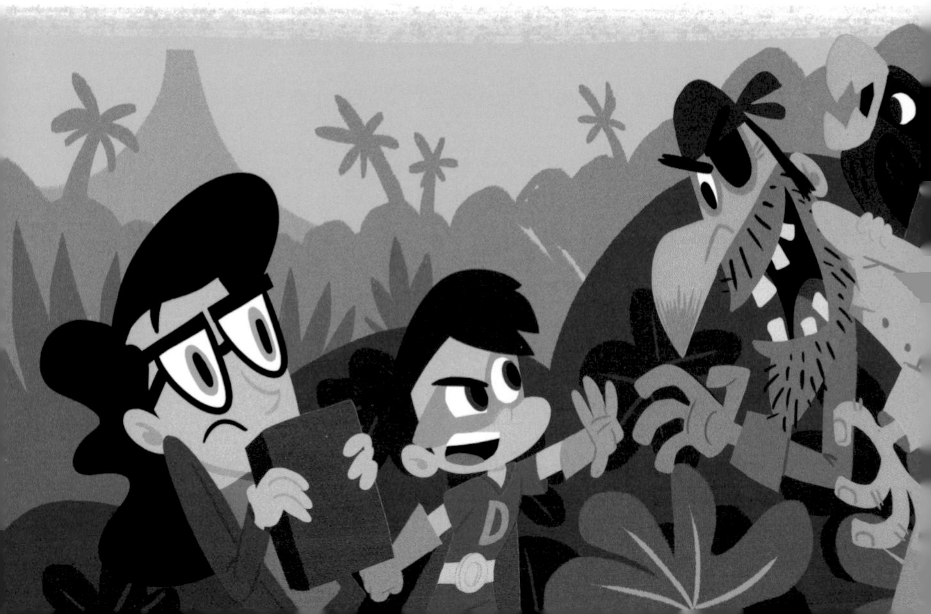
D

Captain Hooksy's voice surrounded them again. "Oh, but *I'm* telling the story now, Booksy, and I don't think you'll like this next part!"

Long John Silver pointed the tip of his sharp sword right at Ms. Booksy and Drew. "Maybe we should board my ship," he snarled, "and take a little walk on the plank!"

"Walk the plank! Walk the plank!" repeated the parrot. **"SQUAWK!"**

CHAPTER FIVE

MS. BOOKSY leaned over and whispered, "Drew, I think this might be a very good time to ***draw something*** with that ***mighty Pen Ultimate*** of yours."

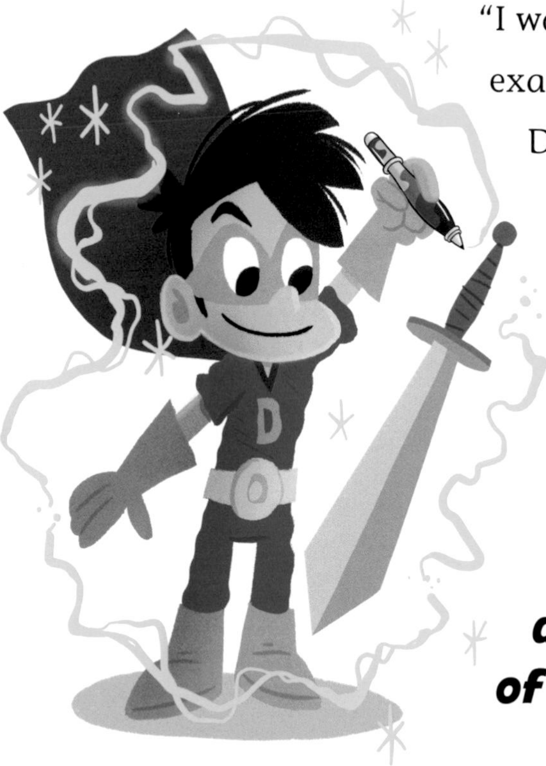

D

"I was thinking the exact same thing," Drew whispered back. He quickly drew himself a long, gleaming sword.

"There!" he said. ***"What do you think of that?"***

"I'll tell you what I think," Captain Hooksy said from the Cool School library. "I think all the **scary pirates** have long, sharp swords, too! Looks like you're outnumbered, Drew Pendous!"

ZHHWWWINNNG! All the pirates yanked their swords out from their belts, ready for a swordfight!

"Um, maybe I should have a sword, too," Ms. Booksy suggested.

"Oh, sorry, Ms. Booksy," Drew apologized. "I should have thought of that! Here you go!" He sketched **another sword** and handed it to Ms. Booksy.

"Yahrrrrr!" the pirates growled, moving forward.

Drew saw that he and Ms. Booksy were still outnumbered. **"Time out!"** he cried.

The pirates hesitated, not sure what "time out" meant.

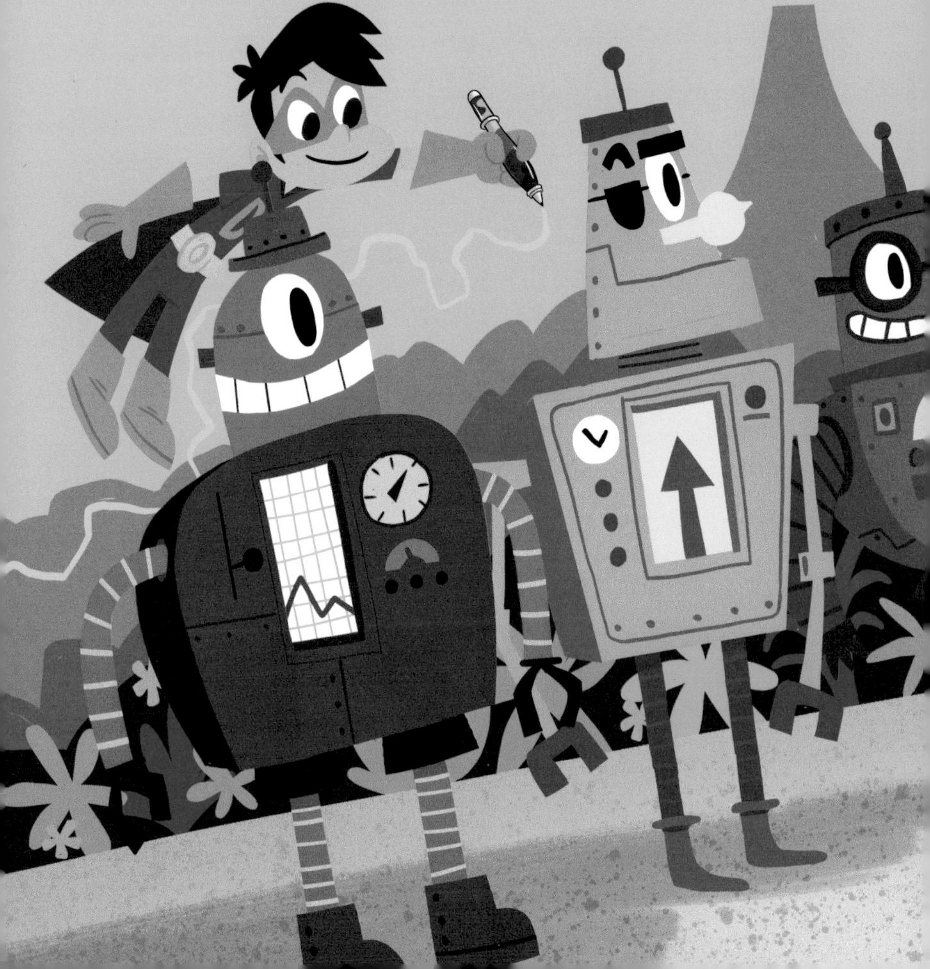

"We're gonna need some backup," Drew explained. He flew into action with his ***mighty Pen Ultimate***, quickly drawing three metal figures. The first had only one eye in the middle of his face. The second wore an eyepatch. And the third carried a purple fish.

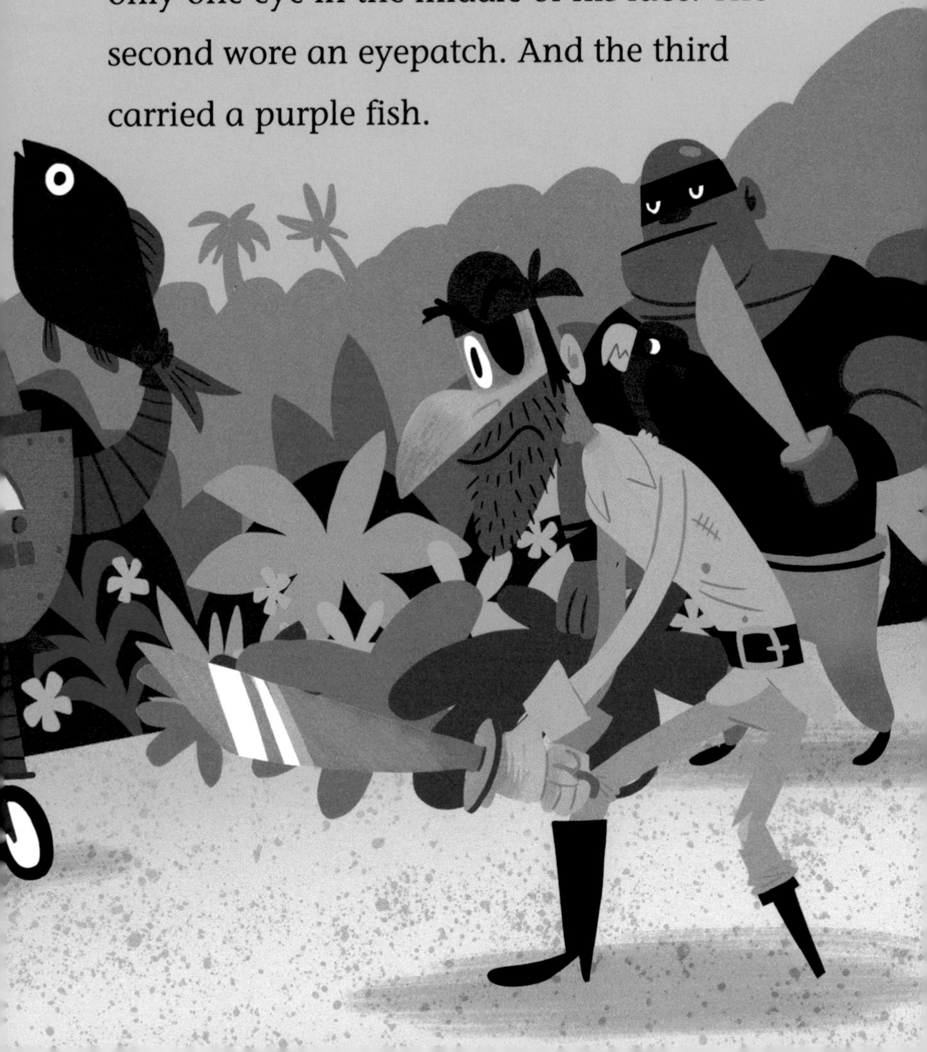

Long John Silver looked confused. "What **ahrrrrrr** those?" he asked.

"Robot pirates!" Drew said triumphantly.

"Robot pirates! Robot pirates!" squawked Long John Silver's parrot.

"And they're totally on our side," Drew added. **"The good guys!"**

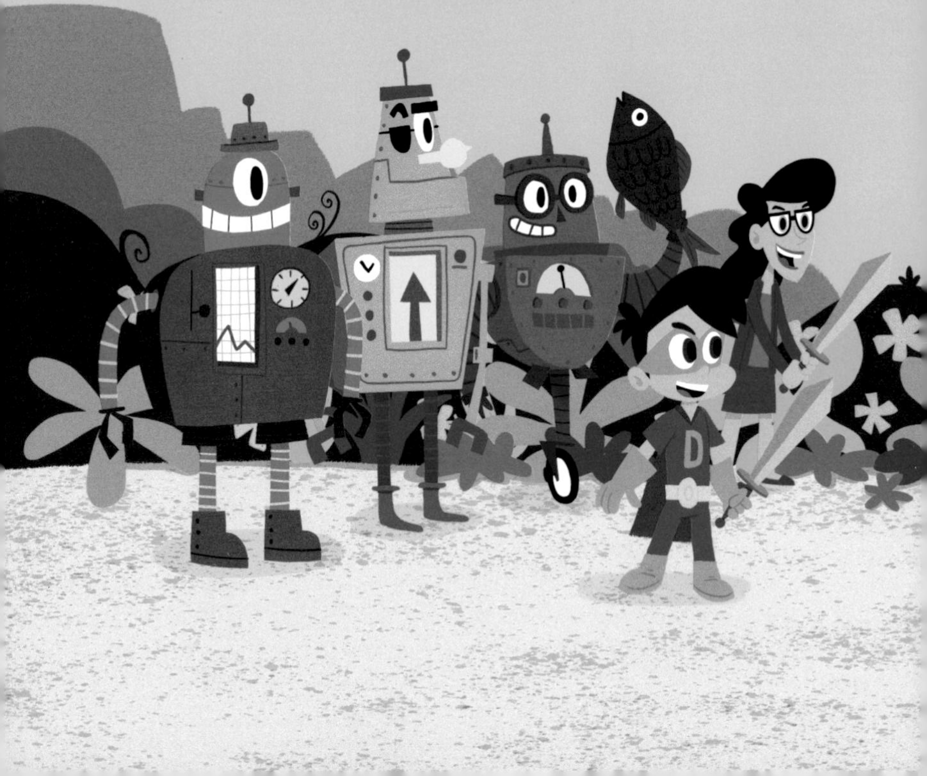
D

The sound of Captain Hooksy's evil laugh surrounded them. ***"Ha ha ha! Good guys?*** In my stories, the good guys ***ALWAYS LOSE!"***

"No way!" Drew insisted bravely.

"There's only one way to find out," Captain Hooksy said. ***"Let the great sword fight begin!"***

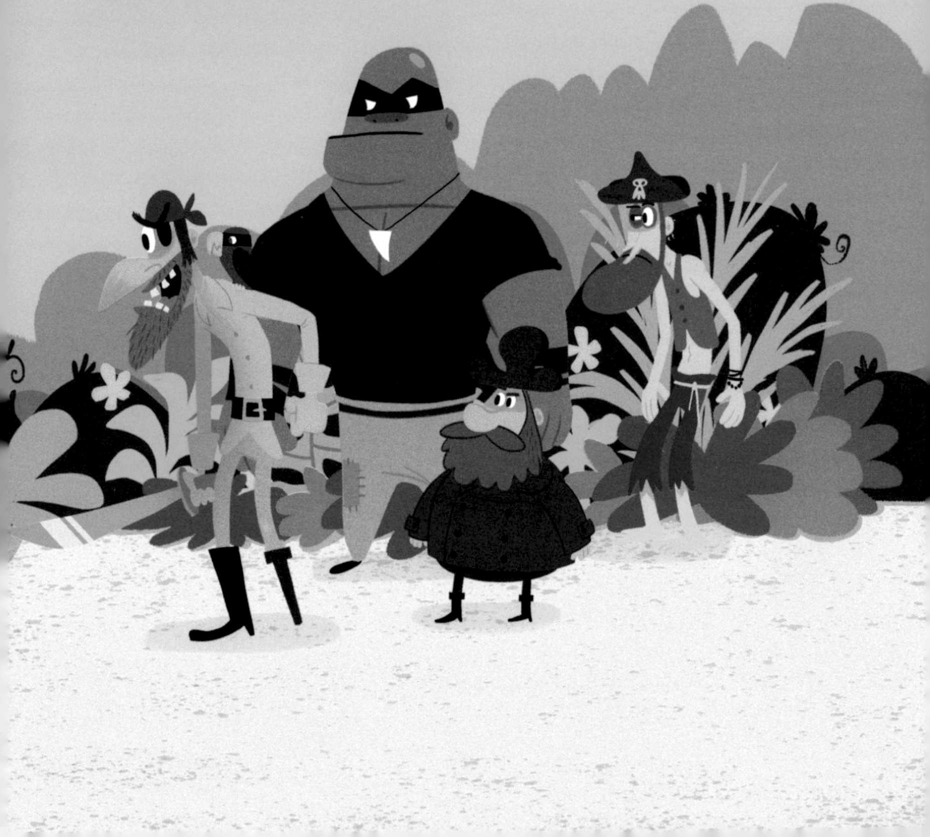

CHAPTER SIX

CLANK! CLANG!

THWACK! The battle began! Swords clanged against swords! On one side were the good guys: Drew, Ms. Booksy, and the three robot pirates. On the other side were the bad guys: Long John Silver and his three non-robot pirates.

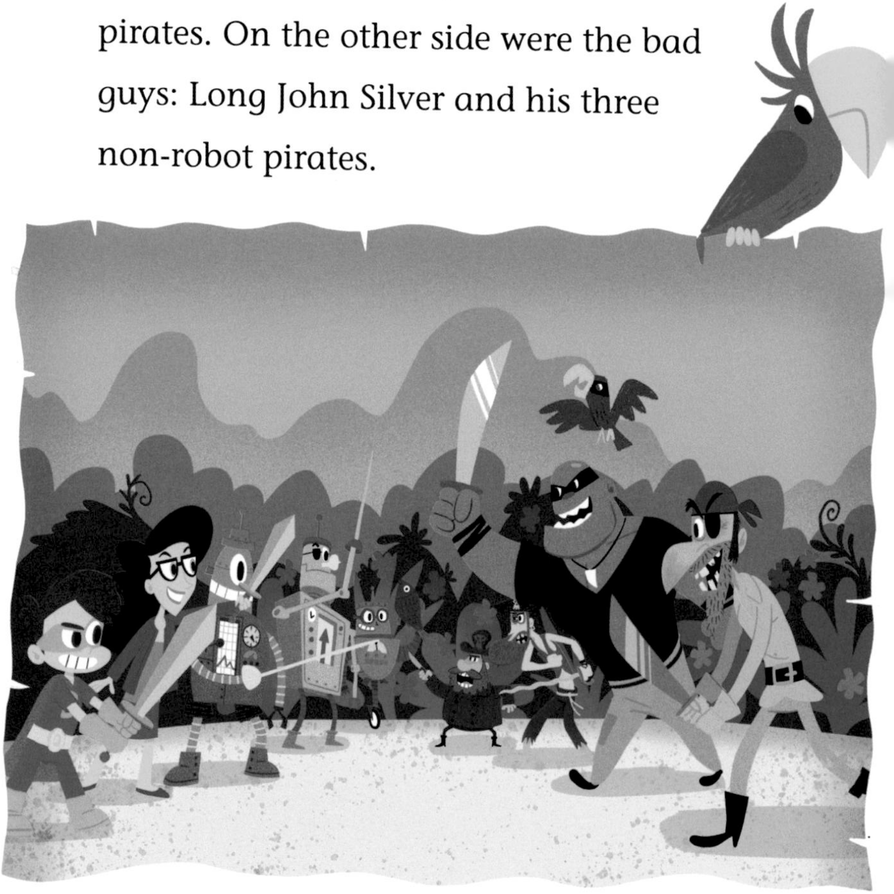

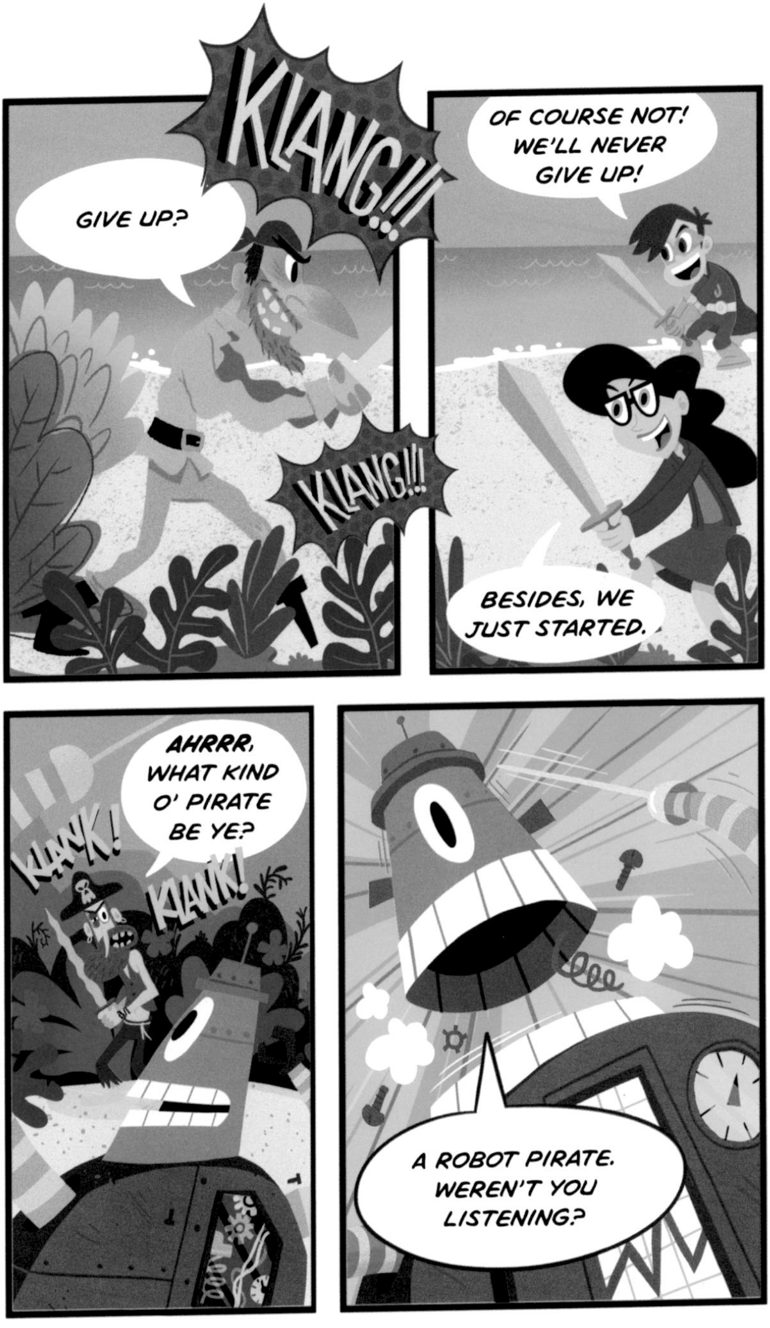
KLANG!!!
GIVE UP?
KLANG!!!
OF COURSE NOT! WE'LL NEVER GIVE UP!
BESIDES, WE JUST STARTED.
AHRRR, WHAT KIND O' PIRATE BE YE?
KLANK!
KLANK!
A ROBOT PIRATE. WEREN'T YOU LISTENING?

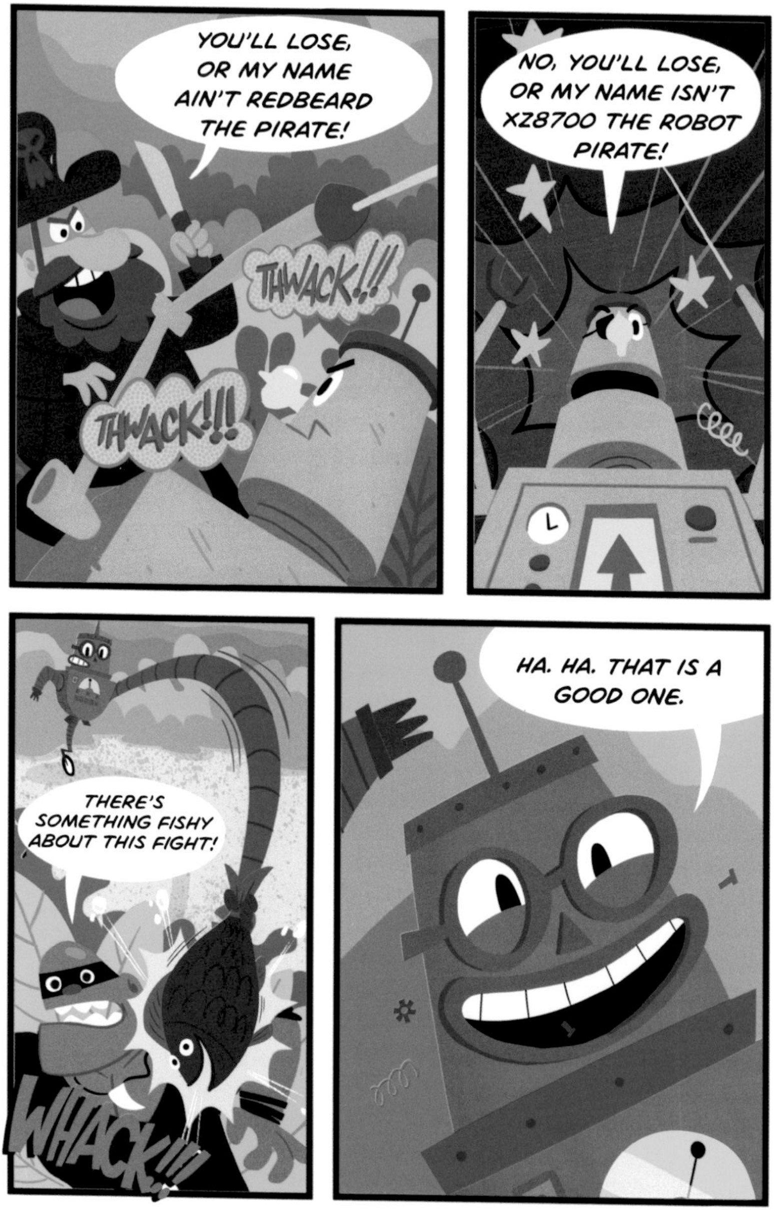
YOU'LL LOSE, OR MY NAME AIN'T REDBEARD THE PIRATE!
THWACK!!!
THWACK!!!
NO, YOU'LL LOSE, OR MY NAME ISN'T XZ8700 THE ROBOT PIRATE!
THERE'S SOMETHING FISHY ABOUT THIS FIGHT!
WHACK!!!
HA. HA. THAT IS A GOOD ONE.

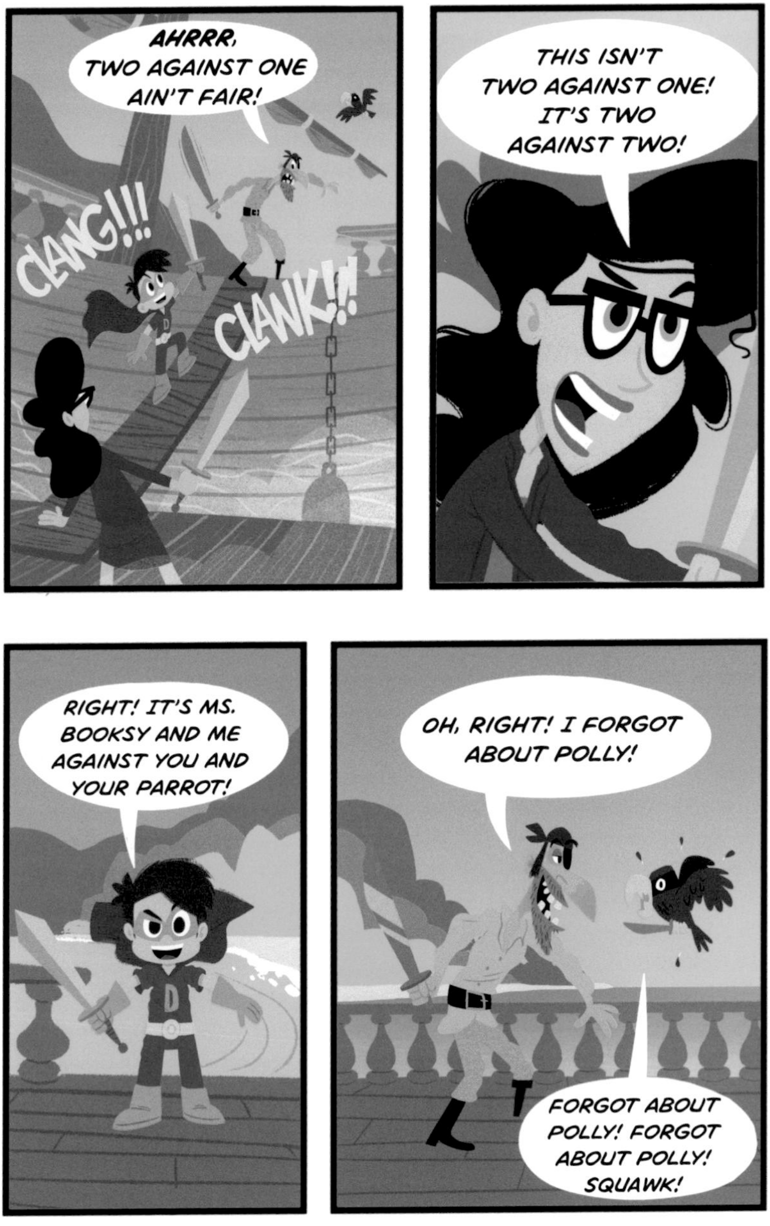
AHRRR, TWO AGAINST ONE AIN'T FAIR!
CLANG!!!
CLANK!!!
THIS ISN'T TWO AGAINST ONE! IT'S TWO AGAINST TWO!
RIGHT! IT'S MS. BOOKSY AND ME AGAINST YOU AND YOUR PARROT!
OH, RIGHT! I FORGOT ABOUT POLLY!
FORGOT ABOUT POLLY! FORGOT ABOUT POLLY! SQUAWK!

Super Drew, Ms. Booksy, and the robot pirates battled Long John Silver and his gang of pirates all the way across the beach and onto their pirate ship! The good guys were winning!

They cornered the evil pirates on the deck of their ship. **"We win!"** Drew said. "That means you have to tell us where the treasure is hidden!"

Long John Silver shrugged. “We’ve been searching for that treasure, but we haven’t found it! We don’t know where it is!”

"Don't know! Don't know!"

squawked Polly.

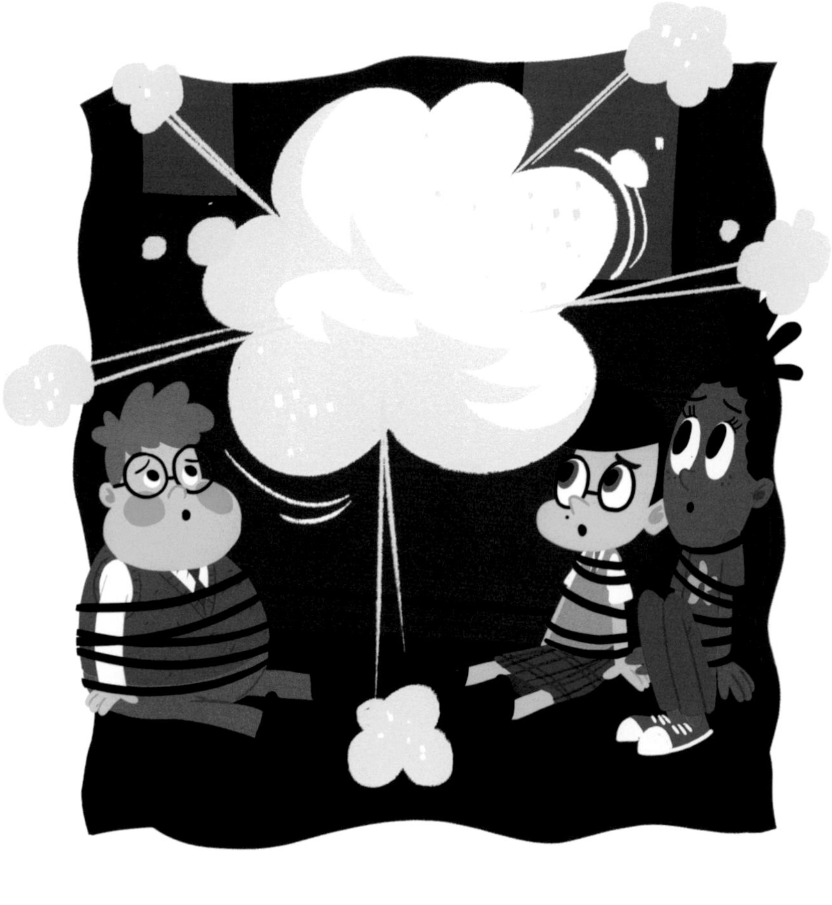

Back in the Cool School library, Captain Hooksy barked, "You seem to be forgetting that I'm telling the story now! And ***this is NOT how it goes!"***

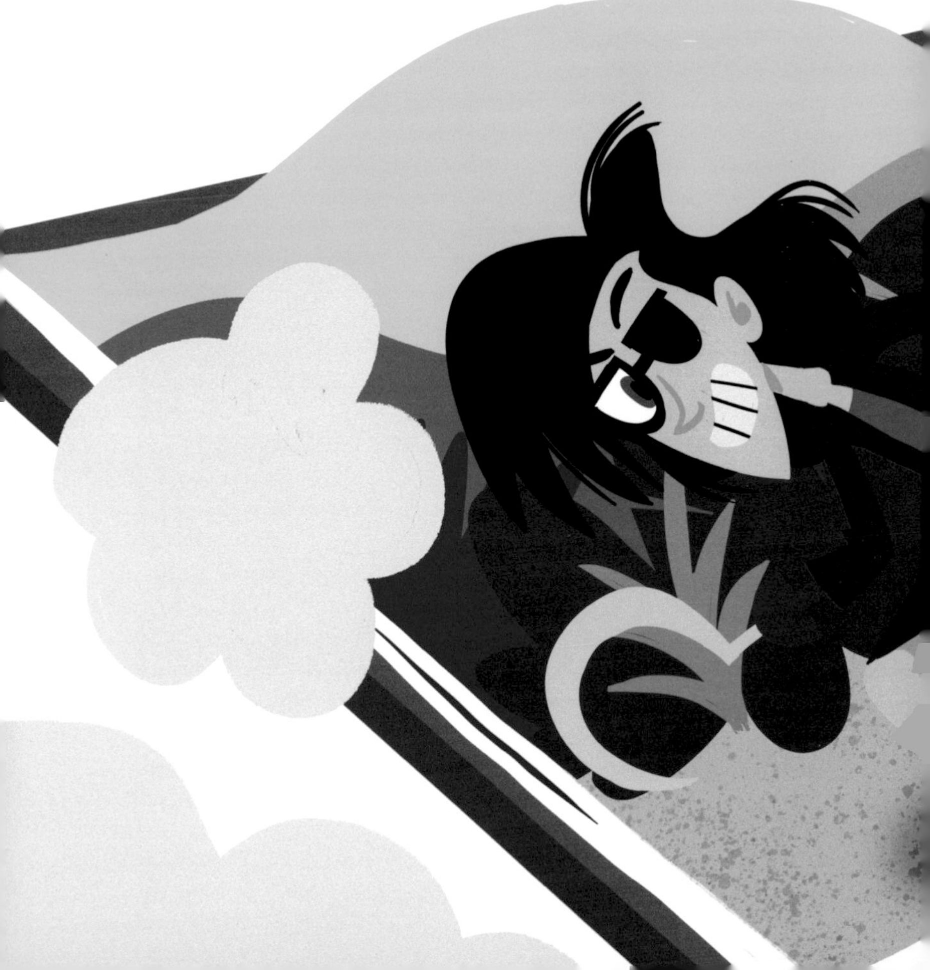

She wiggled her nose and . . . ***POOF!*** Captain Hooksy disappeared from the library in a puff of smoke.

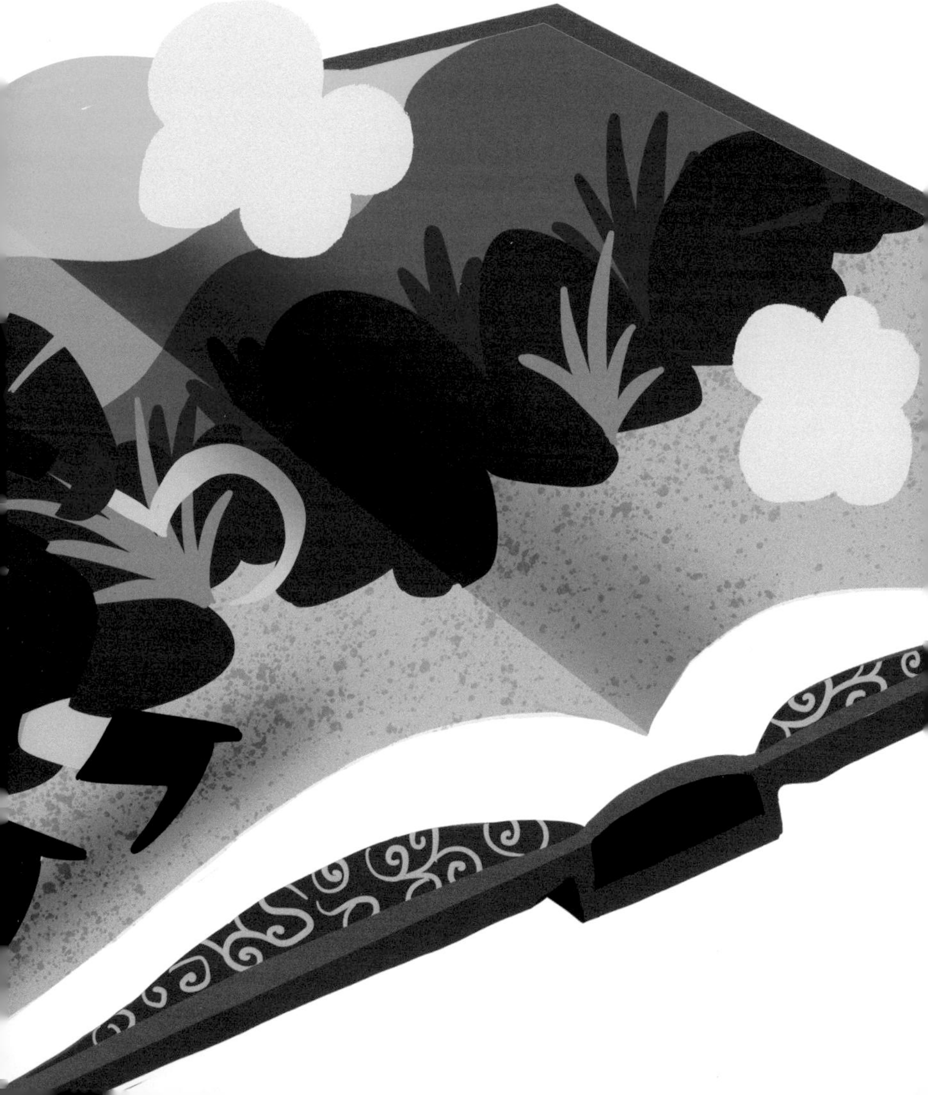

POOF! Captain Hooksy reappeared on the deck of the pirate ship, knocking Drew's robot pirates overboard.

SPLOOSH! When the three robots hit the water, all their circuits sparked out, and they started to rust!

"All right, pirates! The robots are out of the way!" Captain Hooksy shouted. **"Get Drew and Booksy!"**

Long John Silver and his men quickly advanced on Drew and Ms. Booksy, knocking their swords away!

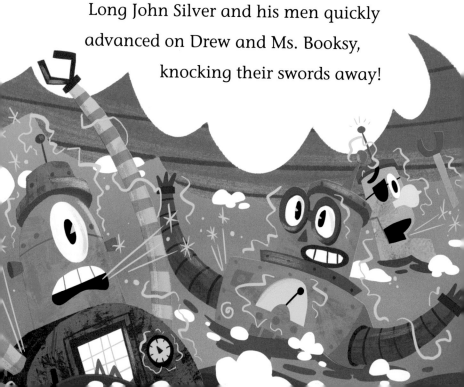

CHAPTER SEVEN

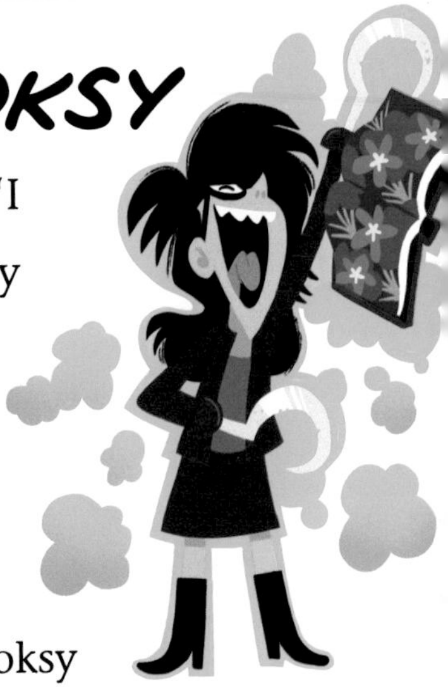

CAPTAIN HOOKSY smiled, satisfied with herself. "I knew that if I wanted this story told right, I'd have to tell it myself!"

"You're a very evil storyteller!" Drew said.

"Thank you," Captain Hooksy said with a little nod of her evil head. "Now, let's get back to our—I mean my—story!" She opened the red book with her hook. "Ms. Booksy and Drew Pendous were captured by Long John Silver and his gang of pirates. Then they were left ***stranded*** on a deserted island—***FOREVER!"***

Captain Hooksy laughed, holding up the book for everyone to see. She was in charge of the story because she had the book.

"Ahrrr," Long John Silver said. "Let's have a bit of rope! A good, strong rope!"

"Good strong rope! Good strong rope!" Polly squawked.

His crew members quickly found a long, thick rope and held it toward Long John Silver. "Don't give it to me, ye mateys!" he roared. **"Tie up the prisoners!"**

"Tie up the prisoners! Tie up the prisoners! **SQUAWK!"**

The biggest, **strongest pirate** grabbed Drew, and **Redbeard** grabbed Ms. Booksy. They dragged them over to the ship's mast (the big pole in the center of the deck that held the mainsail) and sat them down. Then the **pirate with the skull on his hat** ran around them with the rope, tying them to the mast. No matter how much Drew and Ms. Booksy wriggled,

they couldn't get free of the tight rope! After all, the pirates were sailors, and no one knew more about tying knots than sailors.

Drew leaned over and whispered to Ms. Booksy, "You have to ***change this story*** so it has a happy ending!"

Ms. Booksy whispered back, "I'd love to, but ***I can't*** change the story ***unless I have the book!***"

Drew tried to reach his mighty Pen Ultimate to **draw something** that could cut the rope, but he was tied up too tightly. He could barely move! If he was going to get out of this bad situation, he'd have to use his brain instead of his pen. He thought hard . . .

. . . and came up with an idea! He remembered something Long John Silver had told them before . . .

"Hey, Long John Silver!" Drew said.

"What do ye want, ye scurvy dog?" the mean old pirate snarled.

"You're still looking for the hidden treasure, right?"

"I told you we are! Why would I lie?"

"Um, because you're a pirate?" Drew suggested.

"*Hmm,* good point," Long John Silver admitted.

"Well, I know how you can find the treasure," Drew said.

The greedy pirate eagerly leaned in close to hear what Drew had to say. "How? How can I find the treasure? ***Tell me! Quick!"***

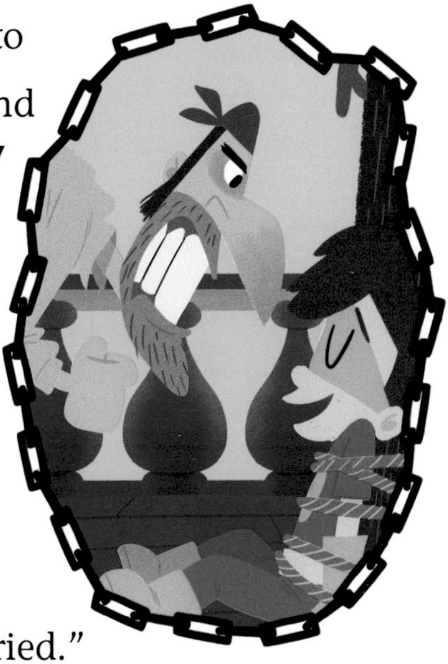

If Drew hadn't been tied up so tightly, he would have shrugged. ***"It's simple. Just follow the map*** to where the treasure is buried."

Long John Silver looked angry. ***"But we haven't GOT a map,*** you fool! If we had a map, we already would have found the treasure and dug it up!"

"Oh, I know where the map is," Drew said casually.

"Where?!" the pirate demanded.

"Where?" echoed Polly. ***"Where? SQUAWK!"***

"It's ***inside the book*** *Treasure Island,"* Drew answered. "If you get me the book, ***you can have the page with the treasure map!"***

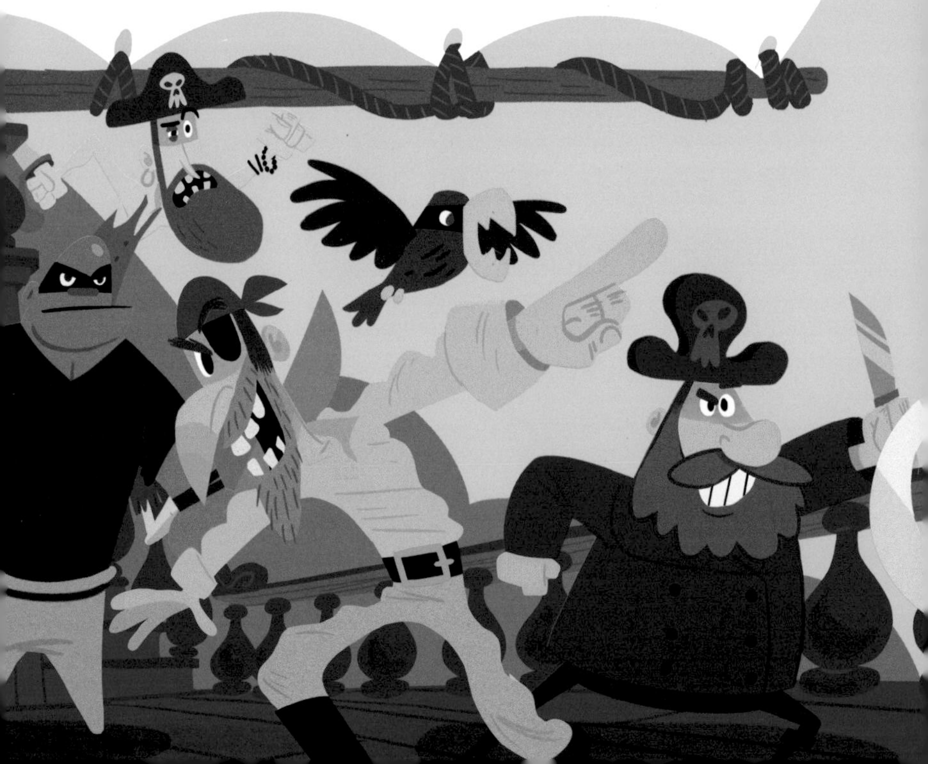

"*Yahhrrrr,*" Long John Silver said with a cruel smile. "That sounds like a deal!" He turned to his nasty crew. ***"Come on, boys! Let's get that book!"***

The pirates pulled out their swords and started walking toward Captain Hooksy . . .

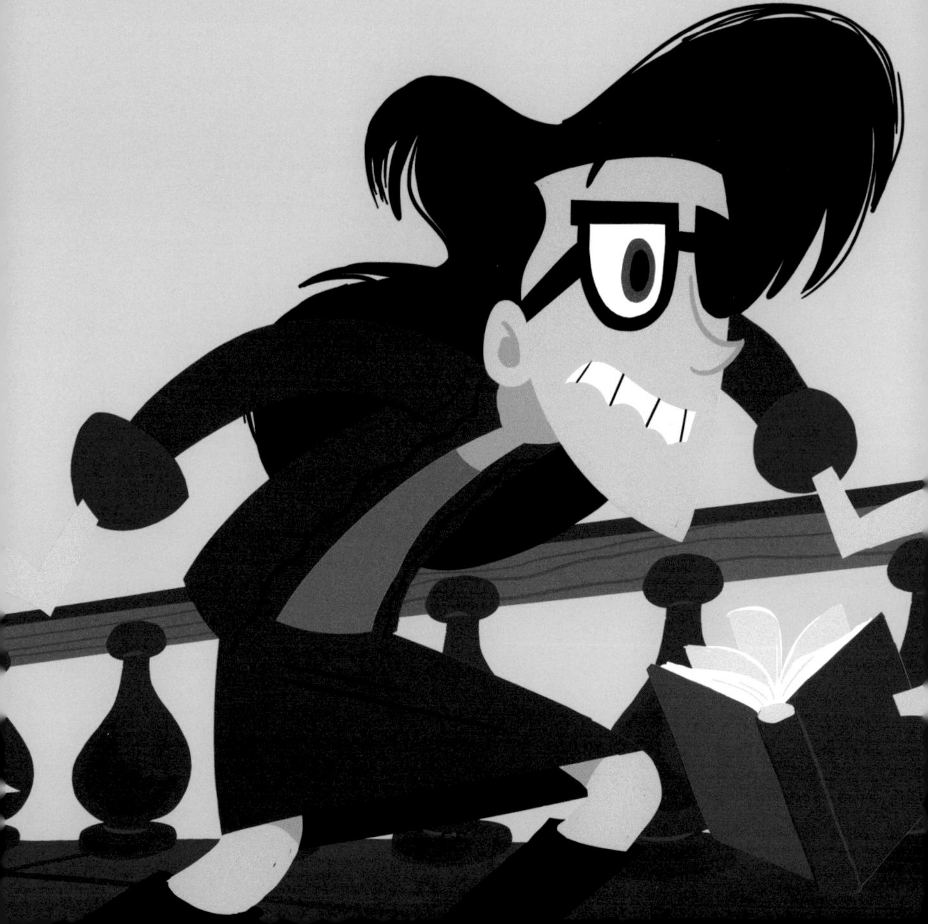

CHAPTER EIGHT

"GET BACK!" Captain Hooksy commanded. "What are you doing?! Stay away from me! ***This is mutiny!"*** But the pirates just kept advancing on Captain Hooksy with their swords drawn.

"We'll be troubling ye for that red book o' yours," Long John Silver said. ***"Hand it over!"***

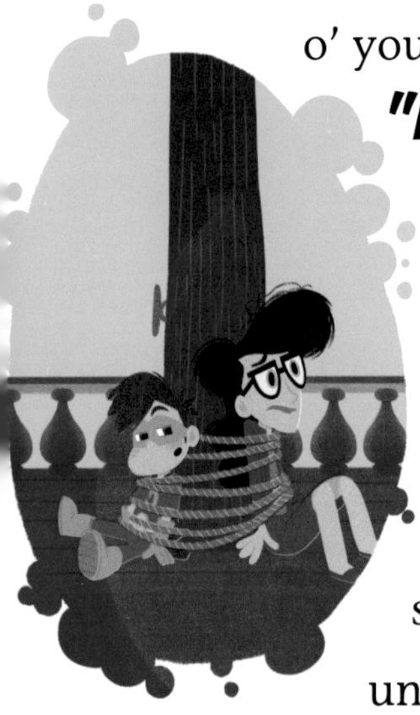

Drew leaned over to Ms. Booksy and whispered, "My plan is totally working!" But Ms. Booksy wasn't so sure.

"Yes, it's working . . . *so far*," she whispered back. "But don't underestimate Captain Hooksy. She may be an evil storyteller, but she's still a storyteller!"

As the gang of mean pirates got closer and closer, Captain Hooksy looked worried. But then she said, **"I've got the book! That means I've got the power over this story.** Listen to what happens next. The pirates stopped threatening Captain Hooksy. Instead, they did exactly what she told them to do!"

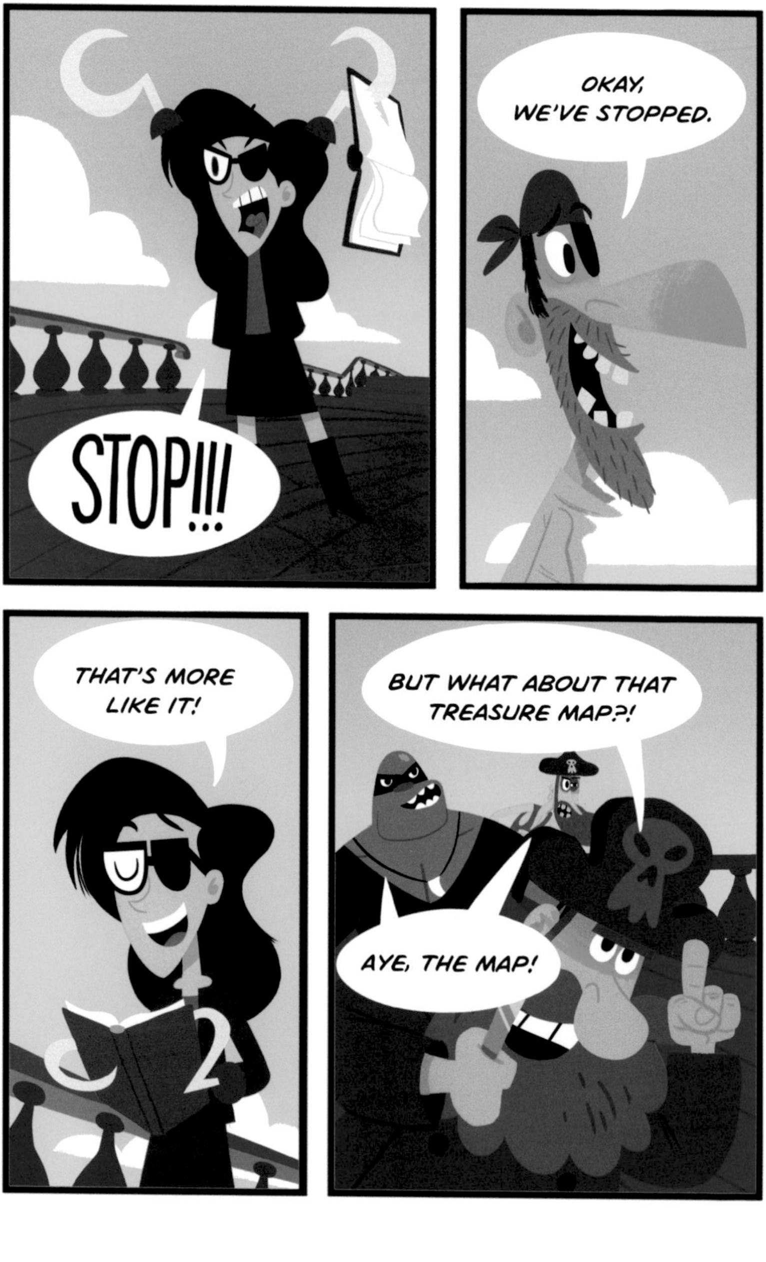
STOP!!!
OKAY, WE'VE STOPPED.
THAT'S MORE LIKE IT!
BUT WHAT ABOUT THAT TREASURE MAP?!
AYE, THE MAP!

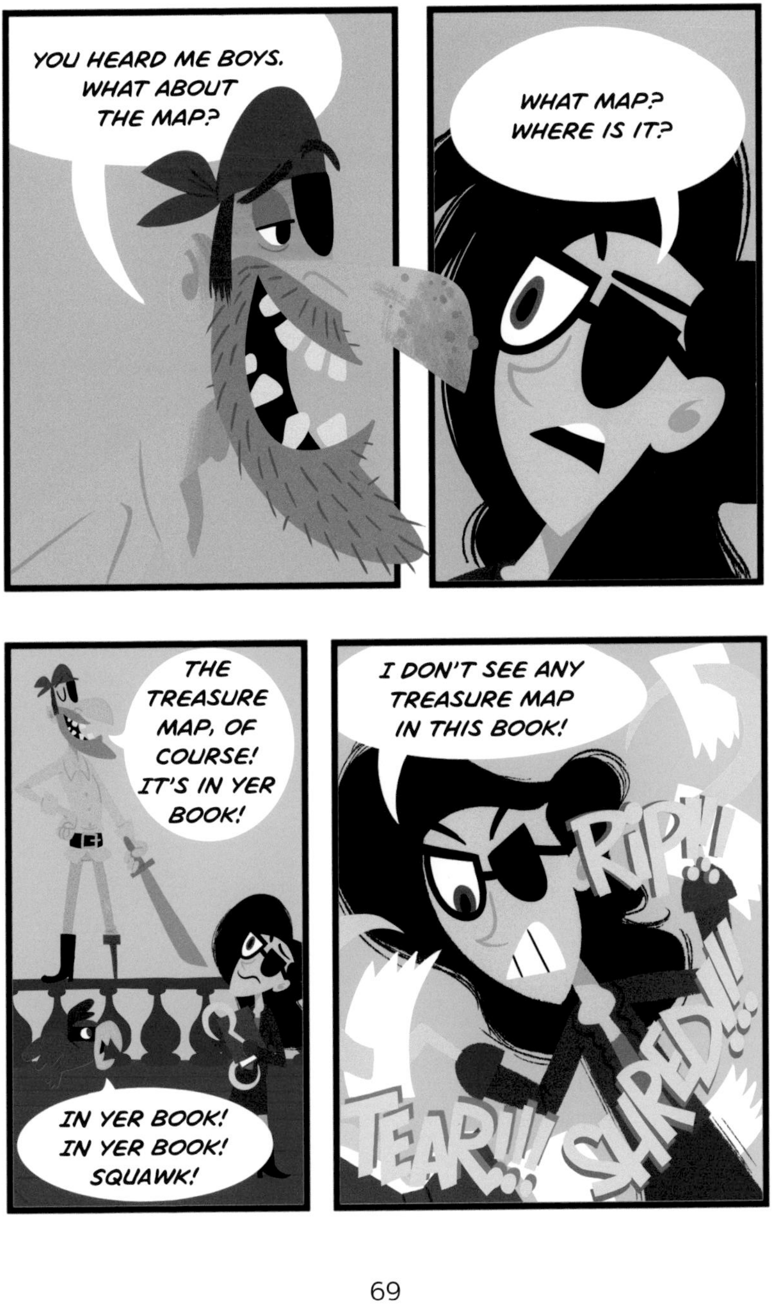
YOU HEARD ME BOYS. WHAT ABOUT THE MAP?
WHAT MAP? WHERE IS IT?
THE TREASURE MAP, OF COURSE! IT'S IN YER BOOK!
IN YER BOOK! IN YER BOOK! SQUAWK!
I DON'T SEE ANY TREASURE MAP IN THIS BOOK!
RIP!!!
SHRED!!!
TEAR!!!

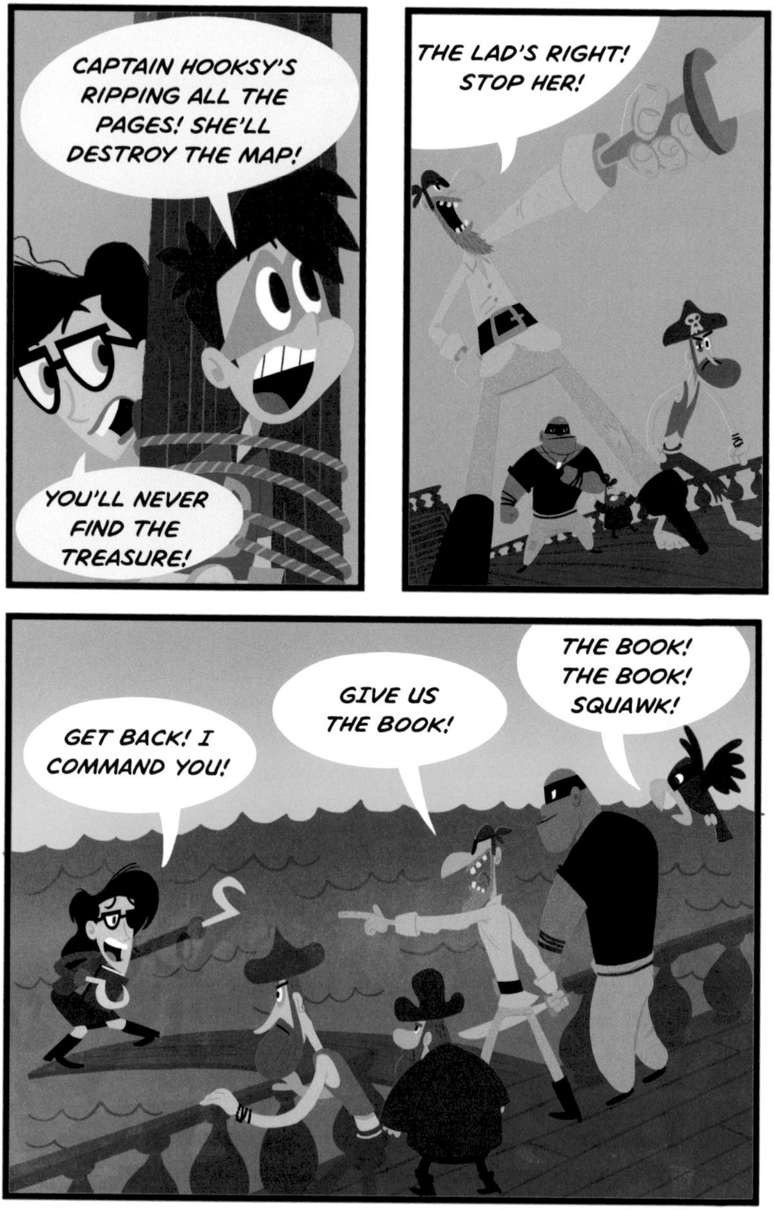
CAPTAIN HOOKSY'S RIPPING ALL THE PAGES! SHE'LL DESTROY THE MAP!
YOU'LL NEVER FIND THE TREASURE!
THE LAD'S RIGHT! STOP HER!
GET BACK! I COMMAND YOU!
GIVE US THE BOOK!
THE BOOK! THE BOOK! SQUAWK!

As she got closer and closer to the end of the plank, Captain Hooksy saw that she had no choice. "Okay, fine!" she shouted. **_"You can have your book!"_**

She tossed the book over the heads of the pirates. They watched it fly through the air . . . and land right at Drew and Ms. Booksy's feet!

SPLASH! The pirates turned back around just in time to see Captain Hooksy leap off the plank and into the sea!

CHAPTER NINE

"QUICK, Ms. Booksy!" Drew said. "Touch the book with your foot, and ***take over the story!"***

"Great idea, Drew!" Ms. Booksy cheered. She stretched her foot until she was just barely touching the red book. Then she started telling the story again, talking

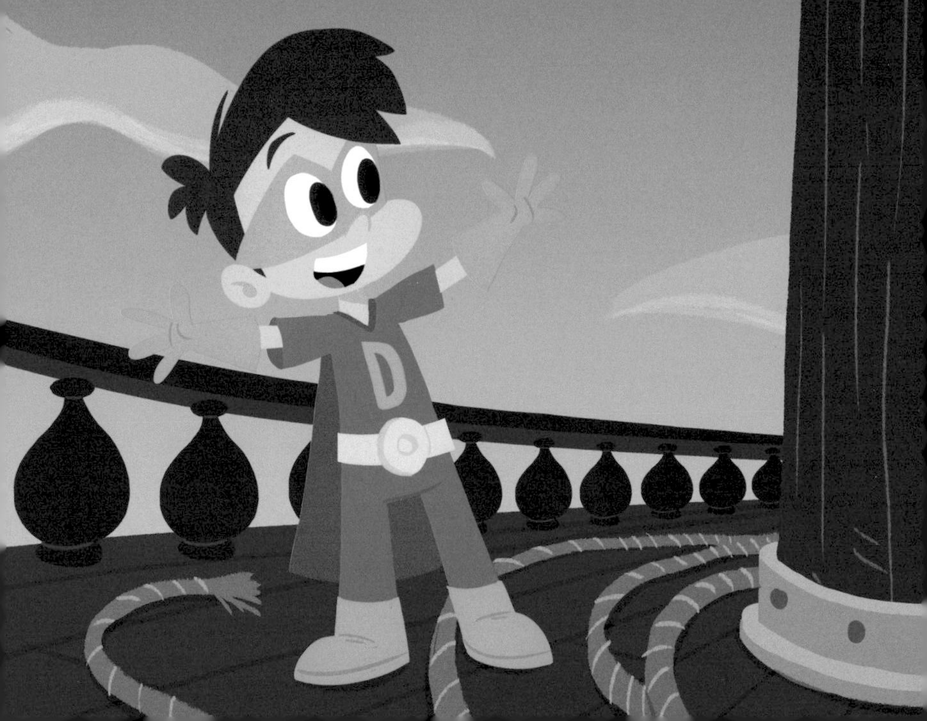

quickly. "By wriggling as hard as they could, Drew and Ms. Booksy were able to get loose from the ropes the pirates had tied around them!"

Like magic, the thick, strong ropes fell away from Drew and Ms. Booksy. They were free!

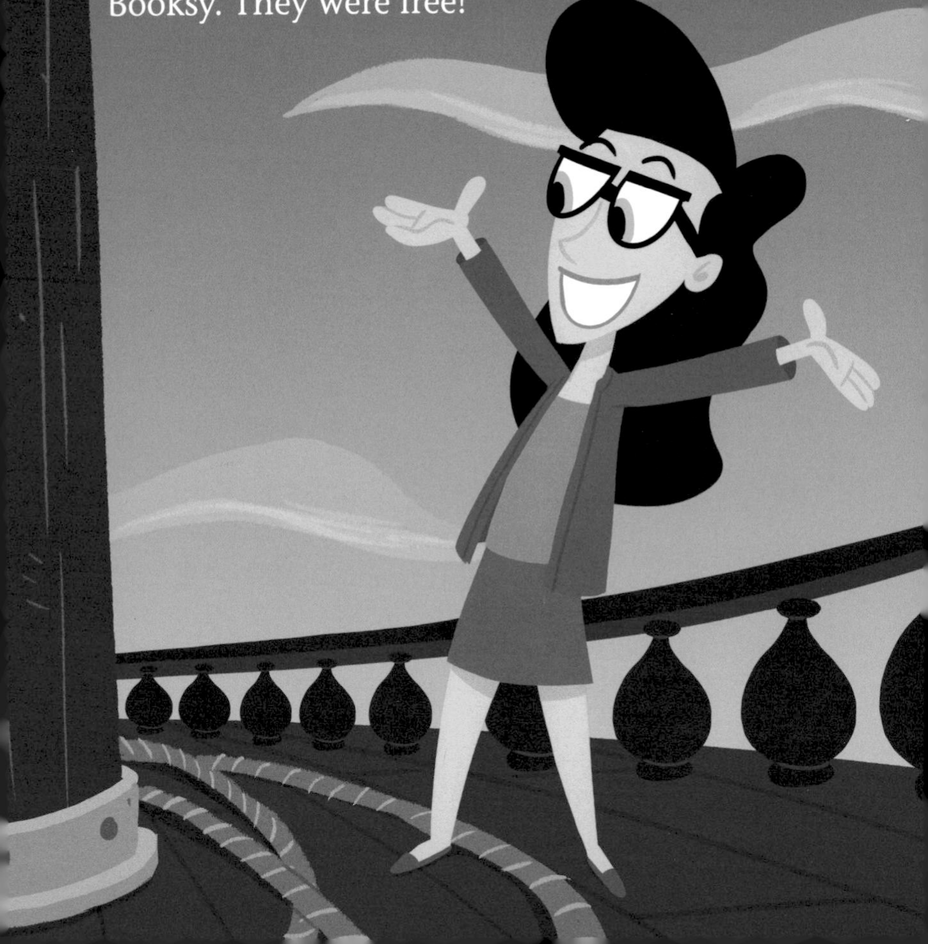

Ms. Booksy hurried to scoop up the red book off the deck before the pirates reached it. She held it tight as Long John Silver rushed up to her. **"Now give me that treasure map!"** he roared.

"Right, um, let's see," Ms. Booksy said as she nervously flipped through the pages. "Treasure map, treasure map . . ."

Drew reached out his hand. **"May I have the book, please?** I think I remember the page the treasure map is on."

Ms. Booksy wasn't sure how Drew could possibly know this, since as far as she knew, he'd never once looked through the pages of *Treasure Island*. But she figured he must have some kind of plan, so she handed the book to him. **"Sure, Drew. Here you go."**

Drew started flipping through the pages. "Well?" Long John Silver demanded.

"Have ye found it? Hand it over!"

"Hold on just a second," Drew said. "I think the light's better over here . . ." He strolled casually away from the pirates and turned his back to them. Then he quickly whipped out his mighty Pen Ultimate and drew a treasure map in the air. **BRRRRING!** Like all of Drew's Pen Ultimate drawings, his sketch turned into a real map!

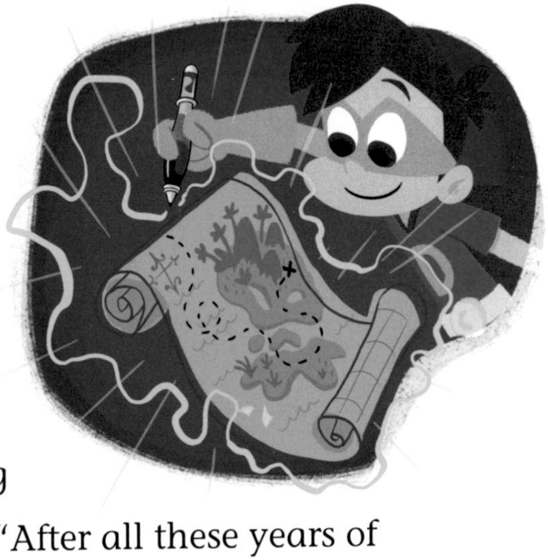

He held it up for the pirates to see. **"Found it! Here's the treasure map!"**

"At last!" Long John Silver cried. "After all these years of searching! **GIVE IT TO ME!"**

"Of course," Drew said politely as he handed the map to the pirate. **"That was our deal!"**

"The treasure map is ours!" Long John Silver announced joyfully, waving the map over his head.

"Map is ours! Map is ours!" Polly squawked.

"HUZZAH!" the pirates cheered.

Long John Silver quickly studied the map. **"Back to the island!"** he cried.

The pirates jumped into the ship's rowboats and rowed back to **Treasure Island** to follow the map and dig up the treasure. Waving goodbye, Drew watched them go. Then he sighed. "I sure would have liked to dig up some hidden treasure. Oh, well. Maybe next time!"

Holding the red book, Ms. Booksy finished up the story. "Thrilled to finally have the map to the hidden treasure, the pirates hurried back to the island.

But having had quite enough thrilling adventures for one day, the really awesome storyteller and the brave superhero returned to **_Cool School."_**

She closed her eyes and wiggled her nose. **_POOF!_** Ms. Booksy disappeared in a puff of smoke.

Drew closed his eyes and wiggled his nose. **_POOF!_** He disappeared, too!

CHAPTER TEN

"OH, GOOD," Drew said as he looked around the Cool School library. ***"My nose wiggle worked that time!"***

"HELP!" cried Nikki, Robby, and Ella, who were still tied up. Drew and Ms. Booksy rushed over to untie the rope and free them.

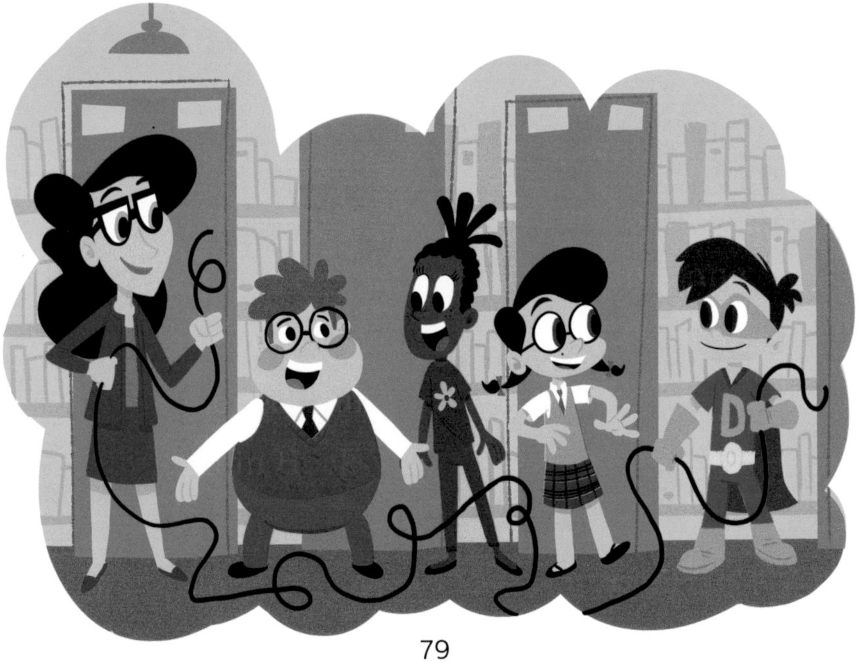

"Thanks!" Ella said, stretching and hopping up and down. "I was getting really tired of sitting in one position."

"And I'm starving!" Robby said. "Did we miss lunch?"

"I don't think so," Drew said. "Let's hit the cafeteria!"

As Drew and Robby headed out of the library, Nikki cried, **"WAIT!"**

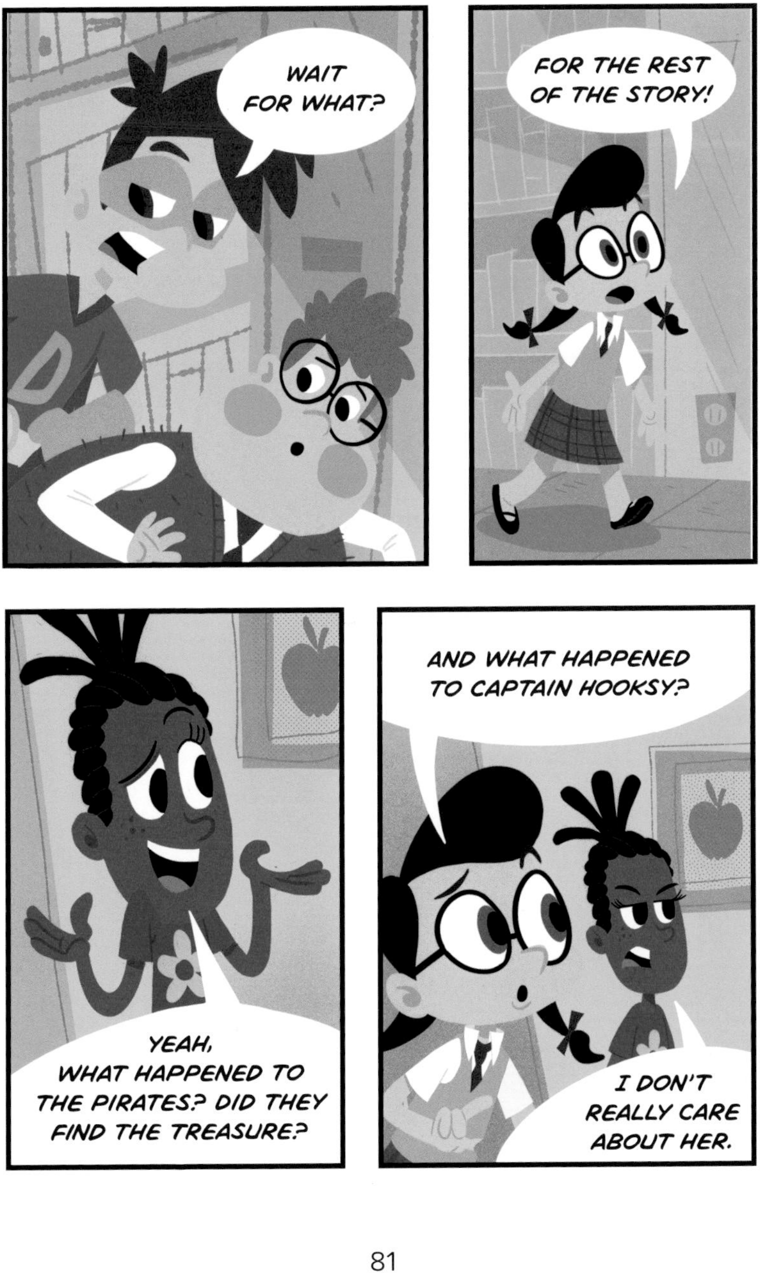
WAIT FOR WHAT?
FOR THE REST OF THE STORY!
YEAH, WHAT HAPPENED TO THE PIRATES? DID THEY FIND THE TREASURE?
AND WHAT HAPPENED TO CAPTAIN HOOKSY?
I DON'T REALLY CARE ABOUT HER.

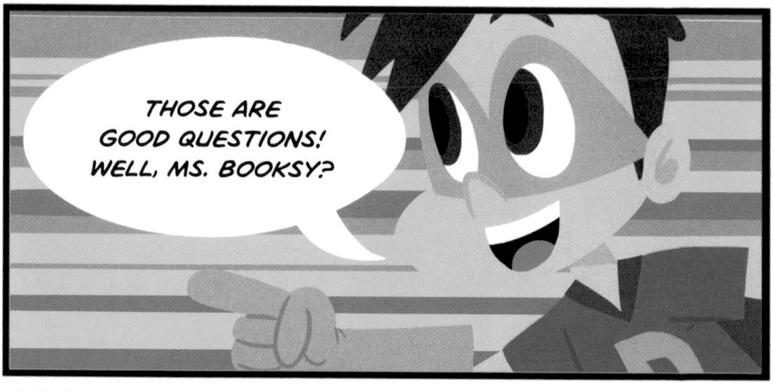
THOSE ARE GOOD QUESTIONS! WELL, MS. BOOKSY?

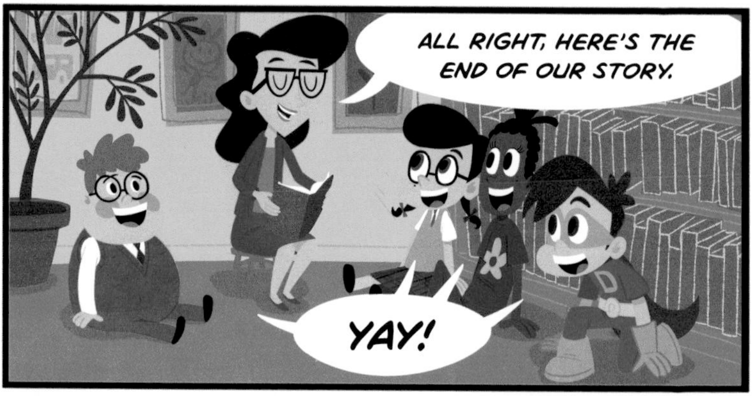
ALL RIGHT, HERE'S THE END OF OUR STORY.
YAY!

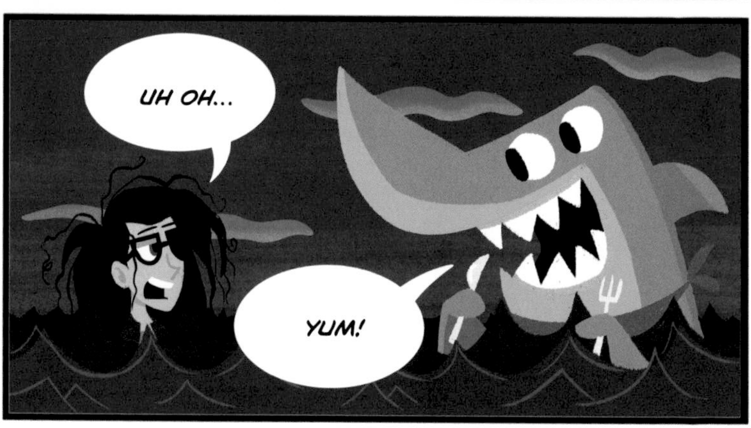
UH OH...
YUM!

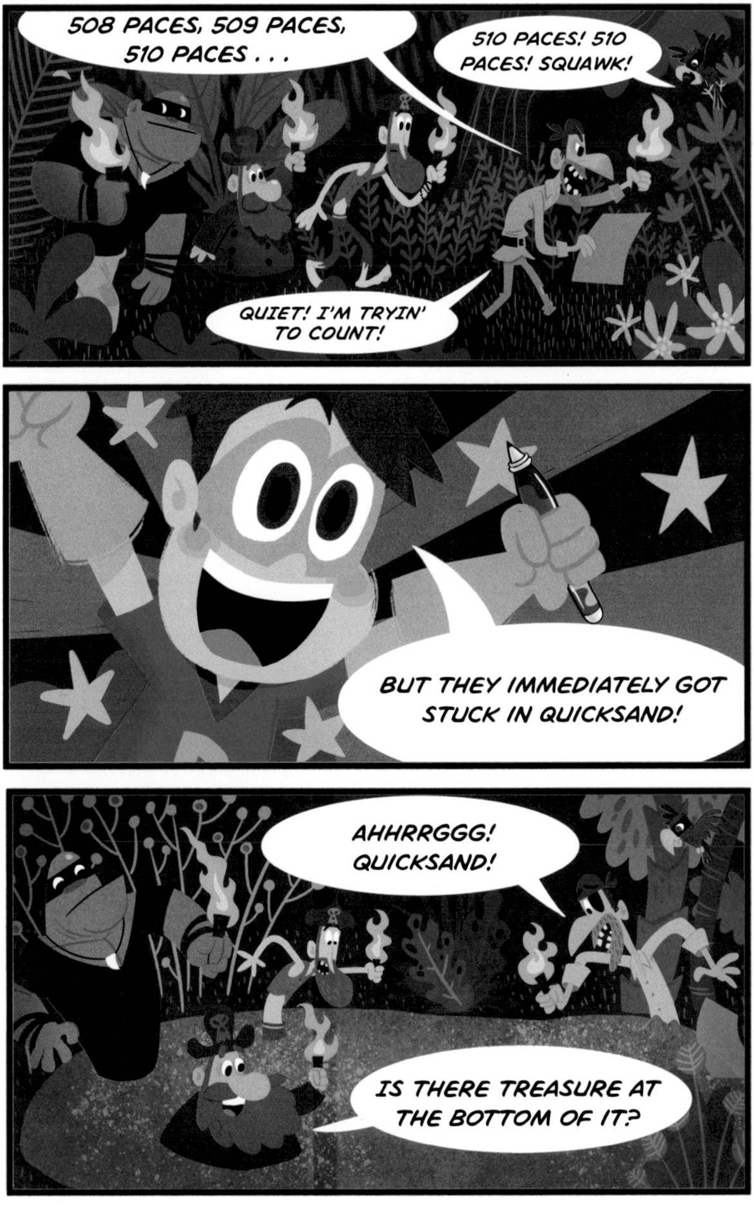
508 PACES, 509 PACES, 510 PACES . . .
510 PACES! 510 PACES! SQUAWK!
QUIET! I'M TRYIN' TO COUNT!
BUT THEY IMMEDIATELY GOT STUCK IN QUICKSAND!
AHHRRGGG! QUICKSAND!
IS THERE TREASURE AT THE BOTTOM OF IT?

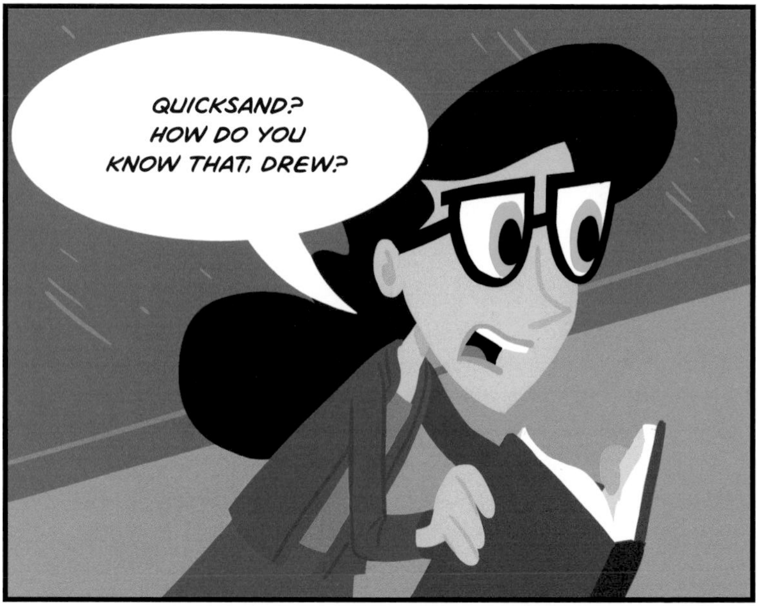
QUICKSAND? HOW DO YOU KNOW THAT, DREW?

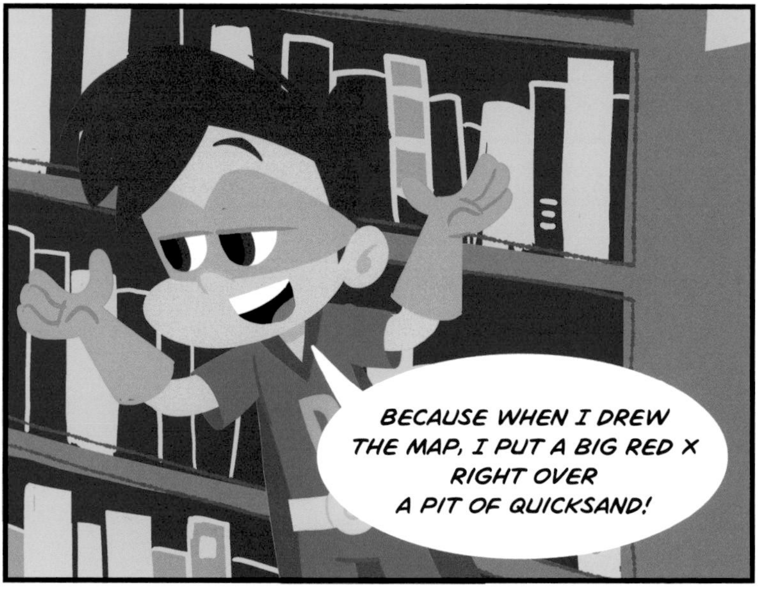
BECAUSE WHEN I DREW THE MAP, I PUT A BIG RED X RIGHT OVER A PIT OF QUICKSAND!

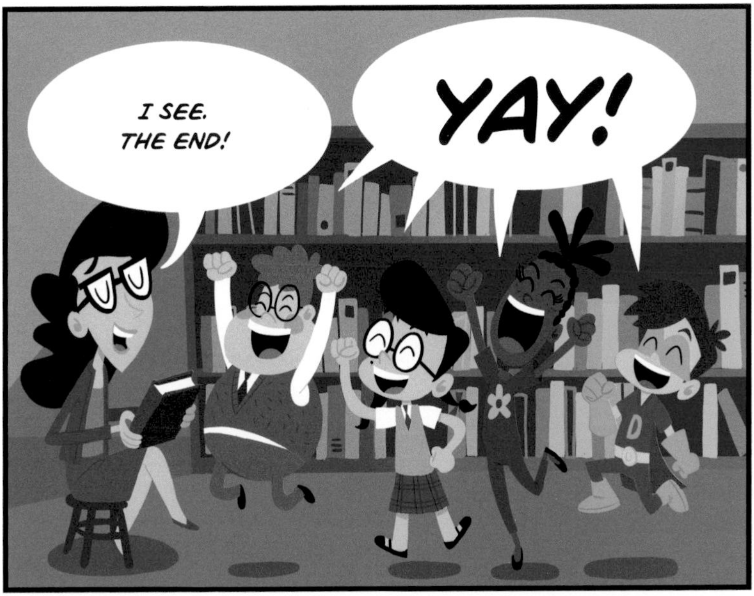
I SEE.
THE END!
YAY!

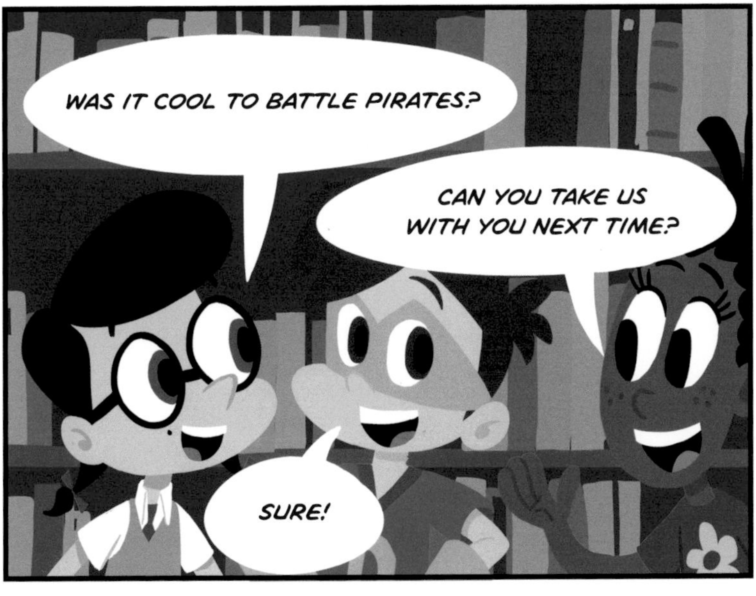
WAS IT COOL TO BATTLE PIRATES?
CAN YOU TAKE US
WITH YOU NEXT TIME?
SURE!

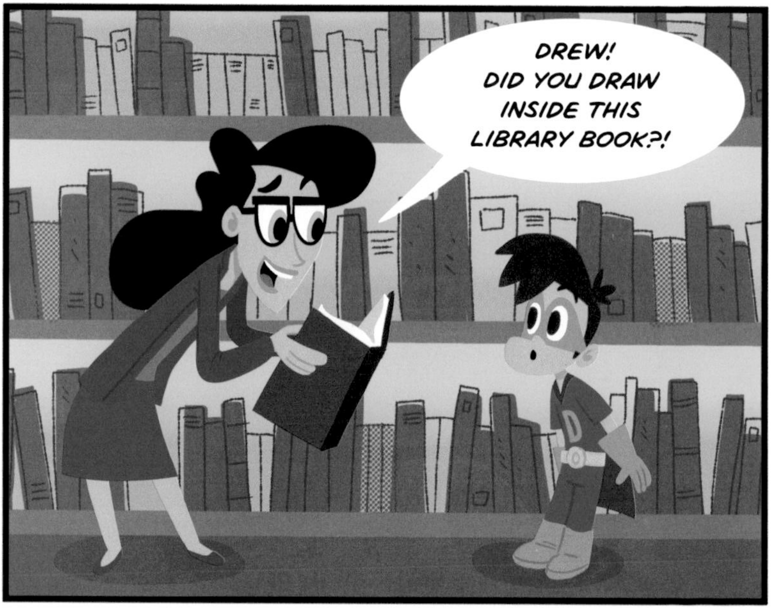
DREW! DID YOU DRAW INSIDE THIS LIBRARY BOOK?!

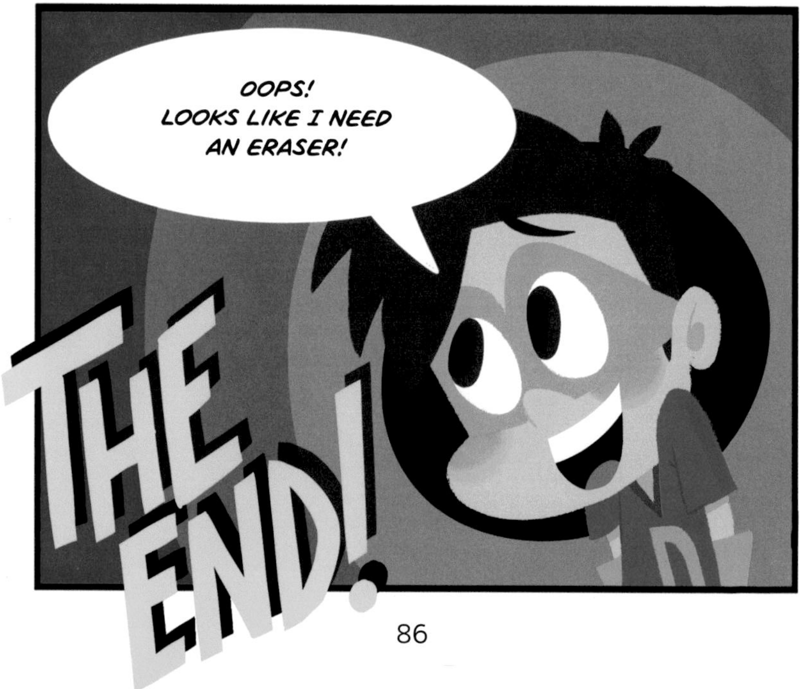
OOPS! LOOKS LIKE I NEED AN ERASER!
THE END!

HAVE YOU EVER

wondered what it would be like to go through a magic portal?

Would you like to read about the coolest summer camp ever?

Does going undercover at Cruel School (but just for a little while) sound exciting?

Then turn the page for:

COOL SCHOOL
DREW PENDOUS
Versus
Ray Blank

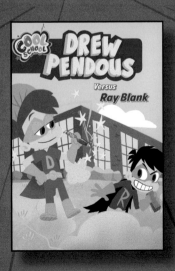

CHAPTER ONE

YES, it's time for another ***amazing adventure*** starring everyone's favorite superhero . . . THE STUPENDOUS DREW PENDOUS AND HIS MIGHTY PEN ULTIMATE!

HI, EVERYONE! YOU'VE MET THE SUPER-NOT-NICE, EXTRA-EVIL RAY BLANK, WHO ERASES EVERYTHING I DRAW, BUT DID YOU KNOW HOW RAY AND I FIRST MET? HERE'S THE TRUE STORY!

Drew and his friends were in the Cool School library. They loved going to the library, because they got to sit on the floor and listen to Ms. Booksy read stories. She was a very good reader. She even did funny voices for all the different characters in the books.

"Good morning, students!" Ms. Booksy said cheerfully.

"Good morning, Ms. Booksy!" they answered.

"I have a special surprise for you," she said.

The kids looked at one another and grinned. They liked the sound of a special surprise!

"Today I am **NOT** going to read you a story," Ms. Booksy said.

The kids stopped grinning. **NOT** read a story?! How was **THAT** a special surprise? It sounded more like a punishment!

"Instead, we're going to make up our **OWN** story!" Ms. Booksy explained. "And we're going to do it together!"

The kids started to smile again. Making up a story sounded like fun!

Ms. Booksy said that she would start the story. Then she'd point at one of the students. That person would tell the next part of the story. When Ms. Booksy pointed at someone else, the new storyteller would take over where the last person left off.

“Understand?” Ms. Booksy asked. “Crystal **clear?** Or clear as **mud?"**

"Crystal clear!" the kids shouted.

“All right!” Ms. Booksy said. “Then let’s start our totally new, **made-up story!**

ONCE UPON A TIME, THERE WAS A . . .
. . . PIRATE!
THIS PIRATE LOVED SAILING AROUND THE WORLD IN HIS . . .
ME? OKAY, UM, IN HIS . . .

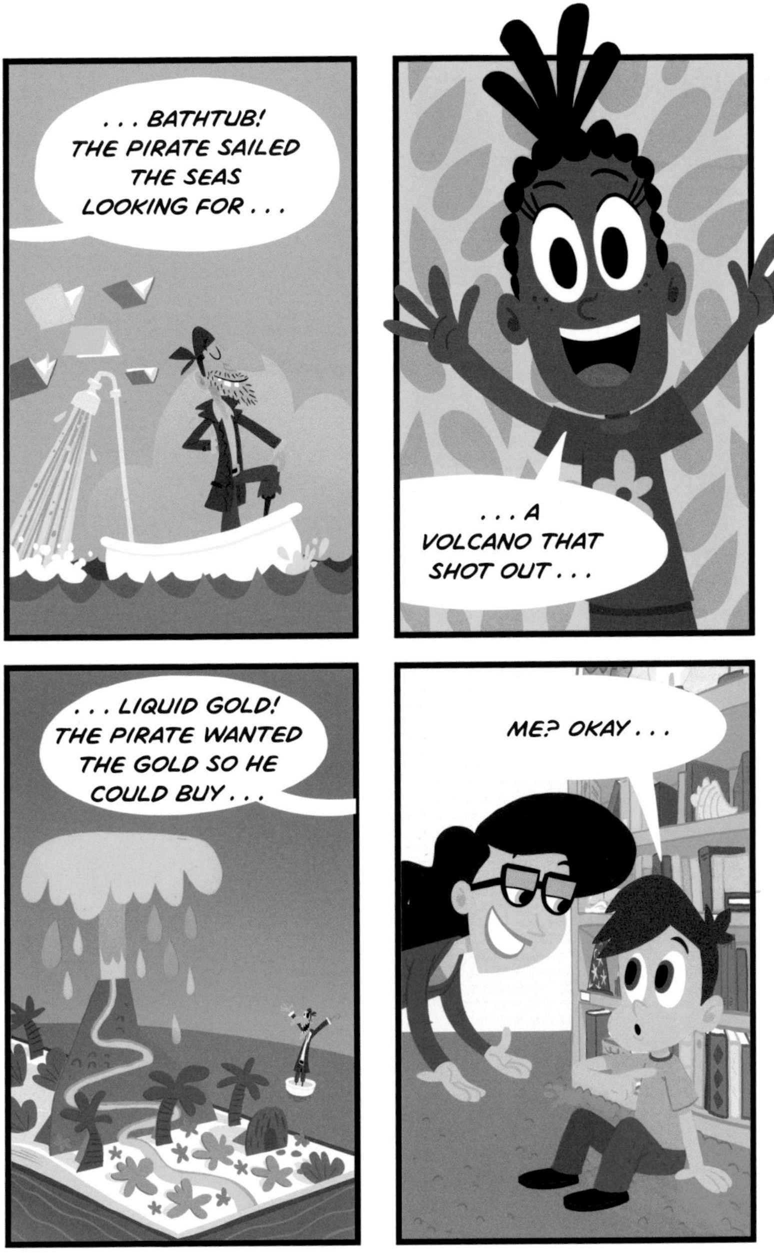
. . . BATHTUB! THE PIRATE SAILED THE SEAS LOOKING FOR . . .
. . . A VOLCANO THAT SHOT OUT . . .
. . . LIQUID GOLD! THE PIRATE WANTED THE GOLD SO HE COULD BUY . . .
ME? OKAY . . .

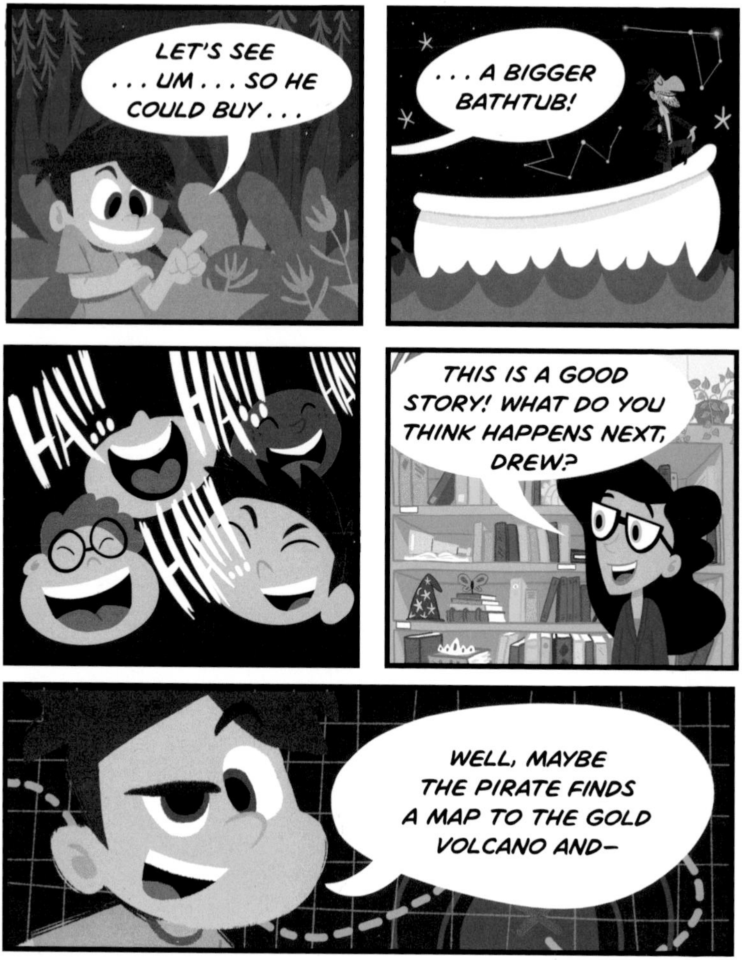
LET'S SEE . . . UM . . . SO HE COULD BUY . . .
. . . A BIGGER BATHTUB!
HA!!
HA!!
HA!!
THIS IS A GOOD STORY! WHAT DO YOU THINK HAPPENS NEXT, DREW?
WELL, MAYBE THE PIRATE FINDS A MAP TO THE GOLD VOLCANO AND—

But before Drew could finish his idea, Akiko burst into the library. "There you are, Drew Pendous!" he cried, pointing his finger accusingly. "Why did you do it? WHY?!"

"Do **what?**"
Drew asked, puzzled.
"Erase my homework!"
Akiko said.

"I didn't erase your homework!" Drew said. "I would **never** do that!"

Akiko didn't look convinced by Drew's denial. "All I know is that my project is **gone,** and I saw you leaving the classroom. At least, I saw the back of you. And you were **wearing a cape!** You're the only kid in Cool School who goes around wearing a cape some of the time."

Everyone stared at Drew. They'd all seen him wearing his superhero cape. Could Akiko be right? Could Drew have erased Akiko's homework?